Fenella-Jane Miller lives in an ancient cottage in acres of Essex woodland near Colchester with her husband, a border collie, an arthritic cat and numerous chickens. She worked as a teacher, restaurateur and hotelier before becoming a full-time writer. She has two grown-up children and two grandchildren. This is her sixth novel.

A DEBT OF HONOUR

Eliza Fox, devastated by the deaths of her father and fiancé, recovers by assuming control of the family estate, firmly believing matrimony has no place in her life. Then Lord Wydale, a notorious rakehell, wins Grove House from her brother, Edmund Fox, who returns to Eliza in the hope that she can save their home. Meanwhile, Mr Fletcher Reed meets Eliza who steals his heart and appears to return his feelings. But can Eliza save her sister and herself from Lord Wydale — and will Fletcher be able to rescue them from the villain?

Books by Fenella-Jane Miller
Published by The House of Ulverscroft:

THE UNCONVENTIONAL MISS WALTERS
A SUITABLE HUSBAND
A DISSEMBLER
THE MESALLIANCE
LORD THURSTON'S CHALLENGE

FENELLA-JANE MILLER

A DEBT
OF HONOUR

Complete and Unabridged

ULVERSCROFT
Leicester

First published in Great Britain in 2008 by
Robert Hale Limited
London

First Large Print Edition
published 2009
by arrangement with
Robert Hale Limited
London

British Library CIP Data

Miller, Fenella-Jane.
  A debt of honour
  1. Regency novels.
  2. Large type books.
  I. Title
  823.9′2–dc22

  ISBN 978–1–84782–630–5

Published by
F. A. Thorpe (Publishing)
Anstey, Leicestershire
Set by Words & Graphics Ltd.
Anstey, Leicestershire
Printed and bound in Great Britain by
T. J. International Ltd., Padstow, Cornwall

This book is printed on acid-free paper

Dedication
For Karyn, my daughter-in-law and Neil,
my son-in-law. I could not have wished
for better partners for my
son and daughter.

Acknowledgements

I would like to say thank you to Robert Foster and Janet Lucas for allowing me to use their wonderful home, Grove House, as the setting for this book.

I would also like to thank the management of the Sun Inn, in Dedham, for giving me the opportunity to explore this historic building.

1

'Eliza, you cannot possibly go outside the house looking like a farm labourer; we are expecting the Reverend Clarkson to visit us today.'

'Mama, I have no choice. I am needed in the barn, the mare is foaling and there is no one else competent to oversee this.'

'But men's britches and your brother's old shirt and waistcoat are hardly suitable, even if you must go and help. I have spoken of this repeatedly, it's not right for you to dress in such a way.' Mrs Fox shuddered dramatically. 'Mama, do you not agree with me? Your granddaughter is making an exhibition of herself. Should she not behave as befits the daughter of a well-respected family?'

Mrs Victoria Dean looked up from the novel she was reading avidly. Her bright eyes summed up the situation at a glance.

'As usual, Hannah, you are overreacting. Eliza has a job to do and, unlike anyone else in this godforsaken place, she is prepared to do it no matter the cost to herself. If your daughter had not taken the estate in hand when your husband drowned five years ago, then where should we be today? In the poor-house, that's where.'

Eliza grinned; she loved her grandmother and she rather believed it was from her that she had inherited her feisty spirit and total disregard for convention. 'Grandmamma, thank you for your support. I am doing no more than I want. After Dickon died I would have fallen into a decline without the occupation I found here. I am merely a caretaker of Grove House and its farms until Edmund comes of age.'

She pulled on a flat cap which fitted snugly over her cropped blonde hair, smiling ruefully as she caught a glimpse of herself in the mantel-mirror. Mama was correct; dressed as she was, it would be hard to distinguish her from one of their workers. Unfortunately she had not been given the regular features and slender build of her younger brother Edmund, nor had she been given the ravishing beauty of her younger sister Sarah. All she had to recommend her was a pair of startlingly blue eyes fringed with dark lashes, a striking contrast to her streaked fair hair. She knew when Dickon had offered for her on her debut, five years before, she had been lucky beyond belief. She had spent every ball, every rout and every party as an overlarge, plain wallflower sitting with the matrons watching the other debutantes dance and flirt with their potential suitors.

Eliza smiled faintly as she recalled the humiliation of being dressed in pastel muslins more suited to young women of delicate features and dainty stature. She stood head and shoulders above most of them and her statuesque figure did not show to advantage in such garments. She never knew why Captain Dickon Carruthers had given her a second look — nobody else had — but one wonderful night, at Almack's, he approached and asked her to dance a quadrille. As soon as his strong, battle-hardened hand had gripped hers she felt her clumsiness fall away and she became one of the chosen.

She had floated around the ballroom radiant with happiness and for some extraordinary reason Dickon had felt the same way. Her eyes filled and she blinked hard to clear them; they had so little time together before he was recalled to his regiment. She had received three letters, three wonderful loving letters, before the final one came from his commanding officer reporting that her beloved fiancé had died a hero's death in a battle somewhere unpronounceable, in Spain.

She had already been in mourning for her father when she received this dreadful news. For several weeks Grove House had fallen into disarray with no one making any decisions. Her mother, prostrate with grief; her grandmother also, at the loss of the man she'd considered as a son. Her brother, at fifteen, away at school untouched by the chaos at home.

Her little sister, Sarah, had been blessed with the most amazing features, like a golden angel, Mrs Turner, the cook often said. However, the good Lord had seen fit to give Sarah an overabundance of beauty but little intelligence. Her younger sister would remain forever a small child, trusting and loving, but unable to function as the adult she now was.

With no one making decisions, rents remained unpaid, the tenants' grumbles went unheeded and revenues from the farms fell drastically. It took the death of one of their labourers to rouse her from her misery; a young man struck on the head by falling masonry in the unrepaired tithe barn.

Enough was enough, Eliza decided. Dickon would not want her to grieve for him the rest of her life. He had died a hero; she must live as a heroine.

From that moment she had taken control and within twelve months Grove House was back to normal, the cottages in good repair and the land also. Crops were sown and cottages cared for and everyone prospered once more. It was about this time that Eliza had decided to cut her hair and adopt men's clothing while she oversaw the farms and estate.

In spite of her mother's anguished protests she did as she pleased. When her beloved had died so had her wish to appear desirable. She would never love another and had no intention of ever appearing at a formal occasion dressed in a hideous pale muslin gown ever again. When her brother came of age next year, he could resume control and then she might reconsider her sartorial decision.

Eliza turned from the fireplace to gaze out across the park and saw a pony and trap approaching the house through the trees that ran either side of the long straight drive.

'Botheration, the vicar is here. I was waiting for Jane to bring Sarah down as I promised she could watch the foal being born. I shall have to go; I cannot risk meeting him dressed as I am.'

'Give me your arm, Eliza dear, I'm not staying in here to listen to that old bore prosing on for hours; I hear quite enough of him on Sunday morning.'

Mrs Fox was shocked by her mother's comment. 'How can you say such a thing? The Reverend Clarkson is a charming old gentleman and does nothing but good in the village. I have promised to help him raise money for the families whose breadwinners no longer have employment on the fields.'

Eliza leant down to offer her arm to her grandmother and assisted her from the chair. The old lady moved with surprising speed for someone of her advanced years and vanished through the wide doors, across the long narrow entrance hall and into the library. She heard the door close with a decided snap.

'Mama, could you send Jane to the stables with Sarah when they do come down?'

Mrs Fox sniffed. 'It is the outside of enough, Eliza, that you spend most of your time up to your knees in unmentionable substances, but now you are encouraging your younger sister to do the same.'

'Sarah has no concept of what is suitable for a young woman of seventeen summers, Mama. She is a child, and enjoys getting dirty and running about freely.'

She hurried from the room and, as she walked towards the back of the house, she heard voices on the stairs and, looking up, saw her sister running down to meet her.

'Liza, Liza, are you waiting for me? I'm just coming. Jane took so long to do up my boots that I am late. Has Princess had her baby yet?'

Eliza braced herself, knowing what was coming next as Sarah launched herself from the fourth step and arrived with a thump in her arms. Eliza swung her sister around — no mean feat, but Eliza had developed a strength that most young women would be horrified to own.

'Come along, Sarah, the vicar is almost upon us. If he sees me like this poor Mama will have the vapours.'

Clutching her sister's hand she dashed to the back stairs that led to the servants' hall. She was halfway down when she heard the front doorbell clang loudly. Mrs Green, the housekeeper, appeared from her small room to answer the summons.

'Good morning, Miss Fox, Miss Sarah, are you going out to the stables?'

'We are. Liza says I'm to watch Princess have her baby; we don't want to see the vicar so we're running away.'

Eliza heard the housekeeper chuckling as she hurried upstairs to answer the door. They kept no male servants in the house as there was no need; a cook, housekeeper, two chamber maids plus two parlour maids were more than adequate. Grove House was a substantial property, but not in the grand style and footmen and a butler, even if they could afford them, would be falling over each other.

The servants' hall was empty at that time of day and she could hear Mrs Turner banging about in the large kitchen issuing instructions to the kitchen and scullery maids whilst she did so.

They exited through the back door which led out into the courtyard. Fred Smith, the head groom and coachman, was waiting anxiously shifting from foot to foot.

'There you are, Miss Fox, I was beginning to think you were never coming down. Princess will not settle without you there beside her.'

'I'm sorry, Fred, I'm here now.'

Sarah snatched her hand away and ran ahead, skipping lightly, her lovely golden curls dancing on her shoulders as she did so. Mrs Fox had been reluctant to dress Sarah as an adult and would have continued to put her in pinafores if Eliza had not insisted it was inappropriate. Although Sarah was a child mentally, physically she was a young woman and it was incorrect that she should be dressed in any other way. In the end they had compromised and Sarah now wore pastel muslins and the necessary undergarments to match, but she wore her hair loose around her shoulders, tied back with a ribbon that matched her gown.

It was dark inside the long brick built

stable block after the bright sunshine of the yard and Eliza paused for a moment to allow her eyes to adjust. She turned to Jane, Sarah's companion and their shared maid. 'Jane, I shall be busy helping to deliver the foal, so you must make sure that Sarah does not get in the way. If she becomes upset take her out at once. Is that understood?'

'Yes, miss, I'll make sure Sarah's good.'

Princess, Eliza's own blood mare, was foaling for the first time. She had been put to a local stallion and Eliza hoped that the resulting progeny would sell at a useful profit.

She could hear the mare moving restlessly in the large loose box at the end of the row. 'Here I am, sweetheart, settle down. You have a baby to deliver; you won't do it unless you settle down and concentrate.'

Tom, the under groom, looked up with a worried grin. 'She's that restless, miss, she'll not push that foal out the way she is now.'

'I'm here, Tom; let me take care of her. She listens to me; all she needs is a little soothing.'

Eliza was quite correct and two hours later, with a final heave, a beautiful filly slithered out on to the straw. The bay mare looked round in surprise at the new arrival.

Sarah clapped her hands with delight. 'Look, Liza, doesn't she look pleased? Can I come and touch the baby now?'

'No, not just yet, darling, Princess must lick the filly clean and establish the bond between them. We must not interfere until she has done that.'

Eliza stepped back making encouraging noises to her mare. She watched with satisfaction as the animal scrambled to her feet and then bent her head to nuzzle at her foal. Minutes later the lovely coal-black animal, balanced precariously on her spindly legs, was suckling strongly.

'Jane, the baby's having a drink. Can I stroke her now, Liza, please, can I?'

Eliza beckoned her sister over and slipped her arm around her waist giving her a loving hug. 'In a little while, darling, the baby has to have a drink first. Then we can both stroke the filly. I'm sure Princess will be pleased to let us do so.'

As she cuddled the new arrival, feeling the softness of its damp coat against her face her heart squeezed with sadness, knowing that she would never have the opportunity to hold a baby of her own in her arms like this.

2

Lord Wydale stood up slowly, his face uncompromising, no sympathy for the young man whose life he had just ruined. 'I shall expect your man of business to deliver the deeds to your properties by the end of the week. Is that clear?'

Edmund Fox kept his head lowered, knowing an outburst of anger would just make matters worse. He nodded once, indicating he had heard Wydale's question. It would do no good to plead that his family home contained his mother, his grandmother and his two sisters; this man had no pity. He had been warned not to enter this room unless he had the wherewithal to cover any losses he made from his gaming.

Flushed with the success of winning a small fortune at another less salubrious club he had thought himself invincible; he should have listened to Wydale's friend. Fletcher Reed had told him not to get in too deep, to stop gambling whilst he could still cover his losses. But he had ignored him, believing, as all do, that good luck would bring him right in the end.

Now it was too late. He had signed away his life in IOUs. He had lost his inheritance, but far worse, he had made his family homeless through no fault of their own. For a moment he was unable to move, his legs and arms refusing to obey his commands. Then, slowly, like a man thrice his age, he pushed himself upright and faced the new owner of Grove House.

'Grove House is home to my mother, grandmother and two sisters, Wydale. They cannot be expected to leave at a moment's notice.'

He watched the other man consider the information, then a slight smile played across his narrow lips. 'That is hardly my problem, Fox. A gambling debt is a debt of honour. Grove House is mine and I wish it to be unoccupied when I take possession.'

'Wydale, consider a moment. I'm sure Fox has every intention of honouring his debt, but it would be gentlemanly to allow him grace to do so.' Mr Reed's voice was well modulated, the words spoken softly, but Wydale flinched as if slapped.

Edmund saw two red spots appear on the man's cheeks and braced himself. The explosion never came.

'You are right, of course, sir. I am in no hurry to possess such a paltry set up, Fox.

You have three months to pay your debt. I shall expect either the deeds or the full amount in cash by the end of July.'

Edmund felt the band across his chest begin to slacken. Three months was not long but, by God, it was longer than three days. He would ride home at once and explain the matter to Liza; she would know what to do. When he had been sent down in disgrace, she had written to the college and he had been reinstated at once. Hadn't she turned the estate from disaster to success? Somehow she would find a way to save them all.

He turned to face the tall, immaculately dressed man, leaning elegantly against the mantelpiece. 'Thank you, sir. My sisters, my mother and grandmother are in your debt.' The man inclined his head a little, but otherwise ignored him. Edmund fled the club in Brook Street and almost ran back to his lodgings in Albemarle Street. His manservant was waiting up for him.

'Denver, we must leave at once. There has been a disaster tonight. I have gambled away Grove House and we have just three months to come about.'

Denver, a man twice his master's age, kept a commendably straight face, not showing the deep shock he must have felt. 'That is bad news indeed, sir, but I'm sure Miss Fox will think of a way out of this disaster.'

⋆ ⋆ ⋆

Fletcher watched the blond young man push his way through the packed room and vanish into the outer vestibule. He was sick of seeing his acquaintance fleece the fresh-faced young men, who appeared every season like clockwork, to dip their toes into games of chance.

'Wydale, I think this time you have gone too far. To take the man's estate is barely acceptable, but to make his family homeless is the outside of enough.'

Wydale's eyes narrowed in annoyance. 'It is all very well for you to cavil, Reed, but you're the warmest man I know. Your pockets are not to let; you could drop ten thousand guineas and hardly notice that you'd done it. I, however, am at *point non plus*. Unless I recoup I shall have the bailiffs at my door.'

'That bad? I knew you'd been dipping deep, my friend, but had no idea things had come to such a pass. Let me help; as you say I would hardly notice a few thousand here or there.'

The two men, one tall, his features aquiline, his eyes and hair dark, the other taller by a head, his hair a nondescript brown, his features pleasant, but not even the most besotted of mothers would call him handsome.

Fletcher knew himself to be no match when it came to charming ladies. He found the business of attending balls and soirées uncomfortable; he did not have an easy fund of small talk ready and knew the many fluttering debutantes and their doting mothers only sought him out because of his wealth.

He hid his discomfort behind a manner that was thought by all, apart from his closest cronies, to be arrogance and did nothing to dispel that myth. When in company he maintained his top lofty stare; looked down his nose from his superior height at all and sundry and they considered him proud and disdainful. Most forgave him because he was rich as Croesus and the most eligible bachelor on the market.

He nodded at his friend. 'It's almost dawn, I think I shall return home and get some rest. I am booked to spar at Cribb's later today and unless I want to lose my bout, I had better get some rest.'

Together they left the club unaware how the crowds parted to let them through. No one, if they had any sense, got in the way of

15

Lord Wydale, who was a deadly shot, or Reed who could floor a man with one blow from his massive fist.

Outside, topcoats swirling around, their beavers pushed firmly on their heads, they strode off to Grosvenor Square, where Reed's magnificent townhouse was situated.

'Reed, I think it wise for me to leave town for a while. I was hardly popular before tonight and once word gets round that I have ruined that country bumpkin I shall be a pariah and my creditors will soon realize I am in desperate straits.'

Fletcher grinned. 'You're a proud man, Wydale. Why not let me pay your debts? Surely it would be better than having the ruination of young Fox on your conscience.'

A bark of laughter greeted this remark. 'Conscience? You know me well enough, Fletcher, to understand that I was born without one. I would rather ruin a stranger than accept charity from a friend.'

'Then let us repair to the country together. I believe that painter fellow, Constable, hails from around Dedham way. I have it in my mind to commission him to paint my estate.' He had made up this idea as he walked; he already had dozens of landscapes and portraits hanging on the walls of his home and had no need for any more, however

16

prestigious the artist.

He was not about to let his friend go down to Dedham on his own. Edmund Fox seemed a harmless enough young man, foolish beyond belief, but harmless. Whatever happened he would not allow the young man's family to be evicted; somehow he would find a way to extricate both men from their monetary problems without either being obliged to sacrifice their honour.

Sometimes he wished he was like ordinary folk — a country squire, a local landowner running his estates — not someone whose ancestors could be traced back to William the Conqueror and whose ancestral home was the size of a barracks and had as much charm as an abattoir. He chuckled at his analogy, and his friend turned to look at him in surprise.

'What do you find so amusing?'

'I was thinking about Longshaw and how much I hate the place. As soon as my father has the grace to turn up his toes, I shall raze it to the ground and build something of a reasonable size which has every modern convenience.'

'Is it the house you hate, or its occupant?'

'Both, my friend, both.'

3

It was almost dinnertime when Eliza headed back; she always changed after a day's work. Whatever her feelings about frills and furbelows she would not dream of upsetting her mother by appearing in men's attire in the dining room.

She hurried upstairs, using the servants' route as usual, and entered her own bedchamber via her dressing room. Jane, was waiting for her.

'I have laid out your royal blue silk, Miss Fox, it's some time since you wore that one.'

'Thank you, Jane. It's a matter of complete indifference what I wear, but I'm sure you're correct, it probably is some time since you put out that particular evening dress. Is my bath ready? No matter if it's cold, the dirt comes off whatever temperature you wash in.'

She strode into her bedchamber pleased to see the hip bath standing in front of an apple-wood fire. It was steaming gently and smelt of rose petals. The screen placed around the bath was more than adequate to hide behind if someone should inadvertently enter the bedchamber whilst she was immersed. It was the work of moments to strip off her dirtied britches, blood-stained shirt and waistcoat. Her boots she had abandoned at the door; she knew better than to track stable dirt through the house. Mrs Green was an efficient and diligent house-keeper and didn't look kindly on anyone adding to her work in such a way.

'Has Miss Sarah gone downstairs yet, Jane?'

'That she has, yes. She was so eager to tell madam about Polly, the new filly. There was no persuading her to wait until you were ready.'

Eliza stepped easily into the deep bath, her long slender legs making the deep sides look shallow. With a sigh of pleasure she sank, ducking her head and rubbing her hair vigorously to remove the last vestiges of straw. She knew that some of the grander houses in the neighbourhood had already installed bathrooms and water closets. Such luxury! What she would give to have a bath in which she could stretch out fully and not be obliged to sit crouched, her knees almost under her chin.

She smiled wryly. Edmund and Sarah were the image of Mama; they had her golden hair, pale-blue eyes and slender frame. Edmund also had her ease and elegance of manner,

19

something she wished she had.

She was the image of her father and some strange quirk of fate had made her the tallest in the family, given her his startlingly blue eyes and streaky blonde hair. Eliza felt a lump in her throat as she thought about the one person who had understood, had always been on her side, and accepted her occasional lapses of what was considered to be acceptable behaviour for a young lady.

He had been returning from one of his many trips abroad when his ship had gone down, taking all hands with it. Although it was now almost five years since the day he had perished she still felt a wrench of sadness every time she remembered.

It was strange, but after five years she could no longer even recall the face of Dickon, the man she had loved so dearly. She remembered the agony she had felt when she'd received the letter. Coming so swiftly upon the death of her father, the double burden had almost been too much.

She stood up abruptly, sending a wave of dirty water cascading over the edge of the bath. She laughed as it vanished through the cracks in the floor. Perhaps one day the ceiling in the parlour would explode, covering everyone with the remnants of her daily ablutions.

Jane handed her a large warm bath sheet and she dried herself vigorously before stepping into her various undergarments. Eliza refused point blank to wear a corset, wearing a chemise and petticoat was torture enough. Obediently she raised her arms and bent her knees to allow Jane to drop the evening gown over her head.

The rustle of silk as it fell to the floor gave her no pleasure. Her mother ordered her clothes from the local seamstress, all she did was specify the colour.

She liked bright colours, quite unsuitable for an unmarried lady, but Mrs Fox was so relieved to have her oldest daughter dressed in anything other than britches and shirts, she allowed her to wear deep blues, emerald greens, damask rose and reds.

Ten minutes after stepping out of the bath Eliza was ready to go downstairs. It was almost five o'clock; the dinner gong would be sounding at any moment. She did not wish to keep her mother waiting. During the day, she did as she pleased, dressed as she liked, spent her time wading through mud, riding astride like a man, visiting their tenants; in the evening she became the dutiful daughter her mother wished her to be.

They were eating the last mouthfuls of a delicious confection that Cook had prepared especially for Sarah when they heard the sound of a horse galloping down the drive.

Sarah jumped to her feet and ran to the window, pressing her nose hard against the glass trying to see who was coming. 'I think it's Edmund. It looks very much like Edmund, Mama. What is he doing here and arriving in such a hurry?'

Sarah ran out of the dining room and down into the servants' quarters where she could escape into the yard. She was obviously determined to be waiting in the stable yard when her brother arrived.

'Eliza, after her quickly. She has no sense when it comes to Edmund. She might well get in the way of his horse and be injured.'

'I think you are underestimating both of them, Mama. Sarah might have limited abilities in many things but she understands animals and Edmund understands her.' Eliza pushed back her chair, knowing it was useless to argue when her mother had made up her mind. 'Are you quite sure you wish me to go outside dressed in this gown? It is doubtful it will survive the experience.'

'Now I have no idea what to do for the best. You have only three dinner gowns; you cannot afford to ruin one of them.'

Eliza hid her smile behind her hand, but her grandmother was not so tactful. Her loud crackle of mirth echoed around the dining-room. 'Hannah, you're incorrigible. Either Sarah is in danger or she is not; whether Eliza ruins her gown should be immaterial.'

Mrs Fox blushed painfully. 'It is all very well for you to make fun of me, Mama, but you do not have the responsibility of clothing my daughters respectably on a limited budget.'

'I shall go down to the kitchen, Mama, and wait for Edmund there. I'm sure Jane is already downstairs and will have gone out with Sarah when she rushed past so precipitously a few moments ago.'

'Of course! How silly of me.' Mrs Fox hurried through the double doors into the drawing room.

Eliza squeezed her shoulder gently. 'I'm sure we're making too much of this. Edmund is a young man, he likes to ride *ventre à terre*.' She smiled. 'I expect he was hurrying in the hope he would be in time for dinner.'

Downstairs Mrs Green was waiting, her face creased with anxiety. 'Miss Sarah ran through a moment ago, Miss Fox, calling out that young Mr Fox had returned. I hope it's not bad news.'

'My brother has certainly returned, Mrs Green, but whether it's with bad news I have no idea. I can assure you that if there is anything that affects this household you shall be the first to know.'

Eliza glanced sideways into the servants' hall where she was relieved to see Jane was not among the girls sitting around the table. Two chambermaids, her mother's French maid, Marie Baptiste, and her grandmother's maid, Betty, were there, all watching through the half-glazed wall to see what was happening.

'Mrs Green, could you send the girls to clear the dining room? I'm afraid we didn't eat the desserts. However, I'm sure they can be served again tomorrow.'

Leaving the housekeeper to return to the small group of women around the table and bring them up to date with what news there was, Eliza continued her journey to the back door. It had been left open, allowing a chill wind to whistle along the corridor. She shivered and drew her cashmere wrap closer around her shoulders. Sarah had gone out in sandals, without a wrap of any sort. The flimsy muslin gown she was wearing would be no protection against the cold April evening.

She was debating whether to gather up her skirt and attempt to cross the cobbles when she heard Edmund's voice, and that of Fred Smith their coachman. Excellent! There was no need for her to venture outside. She

24

waited anxiously in the minimum shelter of the overhanging porchway wondering why her brother had arrived so precipitously.

Eliza watched the archway leading to the stables and was soon rewarded by the sight of her brother hurrying towards the house. His caped riding coat was draped around his sister's shoulders and he had his arm about her waist ready to lift her over puddles when necessary. She was staring at his mud-streaked face, searching for a sign, when he raised his eyes. Her heart sank at the look of desperation she saw there.

Eliza knew without him saying any more what he had come to tell them. She had warned him time and time again to stay out of the gambling hells; that being a man about town did not mean he had to join in all the debauchery and gaming that took place. She knew her words of advice had fallen on deaf ears and, like so many before him, he had believed in his skill and thought that nothing bad could happen to someone whose heart was pure and motives were good.

'Welcome, Edmund.' She raised her hand, warning him not to speak just then. 'Your news can wait. I believe I have guessed why you're here; there is no need for anyone else to know at this point.'

He understood the reference to his sister.

'Denver is following behind with my trappings, but I'm famished, I haven't eaten since I don't know when. Have you finished dinner?'

Eliza, in spite of her fears, smiled. 'Yes, I'm afraid you're too late. However, I'm certain Mrs Turner will find you something substantial. There was plenty left.' She spoke to Jane, who was hovering behind. 'Jane, go in and ask Cook to send up a tray immediately.'

'Liza, Edmund's coat is lovely and warm and he lifted me over the muck so I haven't spoilt my dress hardly at all.'

'Good girl. Now, run along upstairs with Jane, and tell Grandmamma and Mama that Edmund is going to change his clothes and eat before he joins them in the drawing room. Can you remember all that?'

Sarah smiled happily. 'I can do that. I can remember everything and tell Mama about Edmund.'

She watched her sister skip back along the corridor and, as always seeing a beautiful young woman behaving like a child sent shivers of apprehension through her. Her sister was so vulnerable; she wished she had been born plain, and then a lack of intelligence would not have mattered as no one would have given her a second glance.

However, already there were several young

26

men in the vicinity who believed they were enamoured of her sister and professed themselves unbothered by her disability. One of them, the squire's son, Edward Masters, had told her it was part of Sarah's charm.

Pushing such thoughts aside, she turned to her brother. 'I shall come up to your chambers with you. You can tell me exactly why you have arrived like this once we are private.'

★ ★ ★

Eliza paced her brother's sitting room, anxiously waiting for him to re-emerge from his bedchamber in clean clothes. How long did it take, for heaven's sake, to wash one's face and change one's outer garments? She heard the communicating door opening slowly and turned, clenching her fists, waiting to hear just how bad things were.

'Eliza, I'm afraid it is far worse than even you could possibly imagine.' She watched him closely and saw the glitter of tears in his eyes. 'I've lost everything. No, please don't interrupt me. I don't just mean my inheritance, I mean *everything*. The estate, this house, the farms, your dowry. It's all gone.'

Eliza felt her dinner threaten to return and

clenched her teeth until her stomach settled. She collapsed into a convenient chair, ashen-faced, and stared at her brother. 'Edmund, it cannot be? Tell me, not everything? Are we destitute? What about the smaller estate, Hockley House, surely that's not gone as well?'

'Everything. I lost it all to Lord Wydale. His friend, Mr Reed, warned me not to become involved with him, but I ignored his advice.'

He sank into a similar chair and dropped his head in his hands. She had no sympathy. He was a young man; he could join the army, go to the Americas; it was not he who would have to endure the bleak prospect that faced the women in his family. She waited for him to recover, too angry to speak.

He raised his head. 'It could have been far worse. We have three months; it would have been three days but Mr Reed persuaded him to allow us at least that much time to try and come about.'

He watched her, his expression eager, reminding her of the many times she had pulled him out of scrapes in the past. He had come home to her believing that she would be able to find a solution, after all she had always managed it before.

4

Eliza felt despair overwhelm her. It was as if the news had sent her spinning back to the time she was facing the double disaster of the death of her beloved father and her fiancé. They had nothing left if Hockley House had gone as well. She gazed, unseeing, at her brother unable to offer him the comfort and reassurance he craved. She watched him drop his head again in despair. Even a man full-grown needed support and someone to guide him through the perils of being a landowner in an uncaring society.

Watching her brother's shaking frame, seeing him unmanned, made her realize that the fate of the family rested upon those shoulders unless she pulled herself together and tried to give him some comfort. If she was unable to offer even a semblance of a resolution, her brother might do something foolish. She had heard recently that the eldest son of a baron in the next county had blown his brains out on finding himself in a similar situation.

She blinked away the tears of self-pity and straightened her shoulders. They had three months; maybe a miracle would happen and they could find the money to repay this massive debt. She stood up, intending to walk across and offer her brother the comfort he needed, but stopped. Something her father had told her when he had given his permission for her to become engaged to Dickon, something he had said that had seemed odd at the time, but now made absolute sense.

Papa had said that whatever happened she would never be destitute. If she was widowed, left alone in a foreign country, all she had to do was contact the family lawyers in Colchester and they would provide her with what she needed. When she had asked him to explain exactly what he meant, he had smiled and kissed her on the brow. She recalled his words exactly.

'My darling girl, I have invested half your dowry in a scheme that you might disapprove of. However, it will be a lucrative one; if ever you are in desperate need, put your principles aside and be grateful the funds are there.'

She had pressed him to explain, but he had refused. 'I pray that you will never need to access these monies; then they will stay until you are in a position to be able to give them to charity. Forget about this now and enjoy the moment; you have all your life ahead of you. It does my old heart good to see you so happy.'

Three weeks later her father had left and she had never seen him again. Until this moment she had forgotten all about his cryptic comments. Eliza had no idea how much money there might be in this mysterious fund, or what he had invested in that he believed she would not like, but at the moment any money would be a godsend.

'Edmund, it's just possible that there are funds in my name that this scoundrel cannot touch. I have no idea how much it might be, but Papa said if ever I needed them there would be enough to keep me comfortable.'

Edmund sat up rubbing his eyes. 'Why have you never mentioned this before, Liza? Where is this money? How can it be in your name? You were younger than I am now when Papa drowned.'

'It doesn't matter *how*, Edmund, but how much. Wash your face and pull yourself together. On no account must we give the slightest intimation to Mother and Grand-mother that a disaster is about to strike. Is that clear?'

Edmund stood up, his colour returning. 'I understand exactly. We must protect them until we're certain how matters stand.' Unexpectedly he smiled, looking more like

31

the younger brother she adored.

'What shall I tell them downstairs? How shall I explain my arriving in such a pelter?'

'That's easy, Edmund. We shall tell them a little of the truth. Tell them that you have lost a good deal of money and have no funds left to spend gallivanting around town. We must say that you are on a repairing lease until the next quarter. Make sure that Denver supports your story when he arrives.'

The young man nodded, obviously convinced that things would be all right. Eliza did not have the heart to tell him that her father had never expected the money to buy back the estate; it had been intended to support her, and any children she might have produced from her union. She was certain there would not be enough money to pay off her brother's debts, but she was not about to tell him that. Time enough when she knew exactly how much there was. She would contact the lawyers first thing in the morning.

Eliza decided Edmund should ride to Colchester with her summons, believing her brother would be better occupied doing this than kicking his heels around the house imagining the worst. Her mother and grandmother had accepted the partially true explanation of Edmund's unexpected return with remarkable equanimity.

'A young man must sow his wild oats before he settles down, my dear. It is better he does so now, before he has the responsibility of the estate to worry about.'

Eliza had somehow summoned up a smile to answer. 'You're right, of course, Mama, and it will be lovely having him with us until he has come about.'

They were sowing barley in the top field today and she had promised to oversee the job herself. Her man-of-business was busy interviewing new tenants for Cuckoo Farm and was unable to attend to the matter himself. Eliza dressed as she always did when working in fields — a pair of specially made britches, thick cotton shirt and her brother's old top boots. She always wore a coat of her father's to complete her outfit.

Pulling out a cap from an inside pocket where she had stuffed it in the last time she'd worn these clothes, she put it on her head. Although it was now the third week of April, and the trees in many places were in full leaf, there was still a wintry nip to the air first thing in the morning. She rummaged around in her closet until she found a warm muffler and tied it in a loose knot around her neck.

Jane appeared with her charge beside her as she was about to leave. Sarah laughed when she saw what Eliza was wearing.

'You look like a scarecrow, Liza. Can I come with you? If you're going to chase the birds away from the fields I should love to help.'

Eliza felt a moment's doubt. Had she allowed her eccentric dress to go too far? Hastily she returned to her bedchamber to check in one of the gilt pier glasses that stood either side of the mantelshelf. She had to admit she didn't look like the daughter of a gentleman; in fact she didn't look like the daughter of anyone. Dressed as she was she could be mistaken not for a scarecrow, but certainly for a farm worker, or possibly the farmer himself. She viewed herself from every side to make sure that none of her abundant curves was obvious beneath her disguise.

She might look like a young man dressed as she was, but at least no one could say she was showing any part of her anatomy in an immodest way. The top boots covered her from ankle to knee, the britches were not tight and her father's frockcoat fell loosely to her knees. The voluminous waistcoat buttoned across her ample bosom leaving nothing to suggest she was anything other than she wished to appear.

'I'm sorry, Sarah darling, you must stay behind today. It's far too cold to be out. I thought you were going to help Cook make

Edmund a welcome home cake?'

Sarah, easily distracted, nodded vigorously. 'I am, I am. And Jane and I are going to bake buns as well, aren't we, Jane?'

Jane smiled. 'Indeed we are, Miss Sarah, and Mrs Turner is waiting for us in the kitchen this very minute.'

★ ★ ★

Eliza had been riding her father's old hunter whilst her own mare was in foal. Sampson, a sixteen-hand chestnut gelding, well past his prime, would still be considered too much of a handful for most women. Riding astride, as she always did, he was well within her capabilities.

She decided to take the longer route, through the park and across the woods, as it was some time since Sampson had been given the opportunity to stretch his legs and take a few jumps in his stride. She needed the extra time to think about what she was going to do to save her family from ruin. Edmund, as usual, had handed over the responsibility to her and seemed to believe that all would be well.

Lost in thought, Eliza let Sampson choose the path; the way was well known to both of them and included no surprises. She ducked her head automatically as they cantered through the trees and tightened her grip and leant forward when he took a hedge or ditch.

It was unfortunate that Lord Wydale and Mr Reed had decided to walk around the boundaries of the Grove House estate that morning. When the huge chestnut landed in front of them, spraying them both with mud and water from the previous night's rain, a roar of rage jerked Eliza violently back to the present.

Expertly she reined back several safe yards away from the two gentlemen she had just smothered in dirt. The language from the shorter, and more elegant gentleman, made her ears burn. She realized her disguise remained unpenetrated.

'You clodhopping imbecile. You have ruined my jacket with your stupidity,' the man shouted, his dark eyes blazing with rage. The extremely tall man, was scraping the mud from his cheeks, his fine leather gloves being spoilt in the process. She could see his eyes were unamused and for some reason decided that, despite his silence, this man was a more formidable opponent.

Considering it wiser to keep her distance, she attempted to apologize in a suitably countrified manner. 'I begs your pardons, me lords, but this 'ere's private land, and I wasn't expecting no one to be strolling along this path. Was you lost, sirs?' Fortunately Eliza's natural voice was deep and she knew it would not give her away.

The dark man almost growled his reply. 'I am Lord Wydale, and this is soon to be my land. It is you who are trespassing, not us.'

For a moment Eliza was paralysed by fear. How could this man be here already? Had he not promised Edmund to give them three months' grace? The land was not his, not until the deeds were handed over to him. Until then it belonged to Edmund. She was glad now that she had covered both these gentlemen in dirt. It was no more than they deserved.

Drawing herself up to her full height, she stared down at the two men in disdain. 'This land belongs to the Fox family and 'as done for 'undreds of years. I'll not stop 'ere to listen to your nonsense. You 'ave no right to be 'ere and I suggests you bugger orf right now. You might be fancy gentlemen from London, but down 'ere that makes no never mind. It's what you does not who you are what counts.'

Satisfied she'd put them both firmly in their place she clicked to Sampson who was already pawing the ground, eager to continue. Eliza deliberately spun his hindquarters towards the intruders. She dug in her heels hard so that her mount sprang straight into a gallop spraying the men for a second time. The sound of one man's curses followed her and her peal of laughter must have added to his fury. It would take more than a few swear words to intimidate a Fox!

5

Business completed in Home fields, Eliza took the less frequented route home, just in case Lord Wydale and his companion were still wandering around inspecting what they thought would be his property, but not as long as she had a breath in her body to prevent it.

Lord Wydale was exactly the sort of man who would leave his tenants in poverty whilst living in luxury elsewhere. She would not let this happen here; if there wasn't enough money to pay off the debt, then she would have to think of something else. One thing was certain, his lordship would never get his greedy aristocratic hands on her beloved home.

★ ★ ★

She dressed with more attention to her appearance that night. It was possible that they might have unwanted visitors and she wished to look her best. However cold it might be she had decided to wear a new dinner gown, a deep buttercup-yellow silk with a low *décolletage* and elbow-length sleeves. The high waist emphasized her curves and the lighter shade of the gold sarcenet over-skirt shimmered, reflecting the light from the oil lamps around her bedchamber.

'Will I do, Jane? I wish to look my best tonight, in honour of my brother's visit.'

Jane nodded vigorously. 'You do, miss. I don't know why you think so poorly of yourself; you don't have golden curls like Mr Edmund or Miss Sarah, but you have your father's cornflower blue eyes.' The girl grinned. 'And no one could mistake you for a man in that gown, that's for sure.'

Eliza laughed at the oblique reference to the large amount of creamy bosom that was on show tonight. 'I think I shall wear the topaz necklace and ear-bobs that Papa brought from India. Do you know if they're upstairs?'

'They're in the closet, with your other precious items, miss. I'll fetch them right away.'

When the necklace was settled around her throat she felt less naked; she was not used to seeing so much skin; she had abandoned jewellery at the same time she had cut off her long hair. Satisfied she looked as good as she was able, she turned to go downstairs.

Eliza was at the last stair when she heard a

carriage drawing up outside. Surely not? Everyone knew that one did not arrive unannounced at dinnertime, whatever the circumstances. Not waiting to see who might descend from the carriage she ran the last few yards to the drawing room. Three expectant female faces turned to greet her. She glanced across at Edmund, standing by the fireplace, rigid with embarrassment.

Her mother came across and clasped her hands. 'I am so glad you've chosen tonight to dress so well, my love. We have guests for dinner. Edmund met two friends of his from London; they are putting up at the Sun, and he has invited them to dine with us. It's so long since we entertained that I'm quite beside myself with excitement.'

Eliza noticed everyone was decked out in their best. Denver had obviously arrived in her absence for Edmund was in full evening rig and looked every inch a country gentleman, albeit a pale and worried one. Her mother was resplendent in burgundy velvet, a magnificent turban on her head and matching egret feathers dancing and blowing whenever she moved her head. Even her grandmother had made an effort to impress. She had on a strange moss-green velvet ensemble, with an equally hideous turban.

'Eliza, look at this dress Mama has given

me? I feel like a princess. She has put up my hair as well, doesn't it make me look grown up?' Sarah twirled around, delighted with her new finery.

Eliza felt sick with dread. Indeed her lovely young sister did look grown up; she looked so beautiful in a simple pink and white striped muslin evening dress, with dainty cuffed sleeves and a modest neckline, it made her heart ache.

She looked as any 17-year-old young woman should look. With her lovely golden ringlets arranged on either side of her face and her pale-blue eyes sparkling with excitement, Eliza knew that a gentleman might find her irresistible.

'Yes, you look lovely, darling, but remember if you are to dine with us tonight, you must not speak unless addressed. You must nod and say 'yes please and no thank you, and how kind' but nothing else. Do you understand?'

Sarah nodded making her curls fly. 'I promise, I promise. I shall not be naughty tonight. If I'm good, can I dress up like this and come down to meet guests another time?'

Leaving her mother and grandmother to discuss the matter with her sister, she indicated to Edmund they should move apart and stand in the deep curve of the bay window to have a private conversation.

'Edmund, what were you thinking of? Have you run mad? Why have you invited those men here?'

Edmund seemed to be having difficulty in answering; he ran his finger round his stock as if it had grown too tight. 'I was returning from Colchester having delivered the note to the lawyers and met them on their way back from a walk. One of our men covered them with mud and they were baying for his blood. When Wydale saw me he turned his anger in my direction. If it hadn't been for Mr Reed's intervention, that man would have reneged on his agreement and demanded that we leave the place at once.'

'But don't you see, Edmund, they will reveal everything? Can you imagine the distress knowing what you have done will cause our mother and grandmother?'

'Mr Reed gave me his word of honour that they would behave as no more than friends of mine from London.'

They heard the bell that hung outside the front door ring and Mrs Green welcoming the two gentlemen in. It was too late for further conversation. It did not occur to Eliza that she was at any risk of being exposed as the country *bumpkin* who had ruined the gentlemen's stroll about the countryside.

She went to stand by Sarah, just in case her sister did something that might reveal her lack of intelligence and cause embarrassment. She was overly protective, but she knew that no one would treat Sarah without respect if she had anything to do with it.

She heard booted feet in the hall outside and Mrs Green opened the double doors. 'Lord Wydale, and Mr Reed, madam.'

Eliza and Sarah curtsied politely, Mrs Dean remained seated and merely nodded, but Mrs Fox moved forward to greet the unwanted guests.

'Welcome, my lord, sir, to Grove House. It is so long since we've seen anyone from London and I am eager to catch up on any news.'

Eliza kept her head lowered, not wishing to make eye contact with either man, in case her animosity was not sufficiently well hidden. She heard Edmund move at last to greet his so-called friends.

'Lord Wydale, allow me to present my mother, Mrs Fox.' There was the sound of bowing and curtseying, but Eliza remained where she was.

'This is my grandmother, Mrs Dean.'

She risked a glance, eager to see how her eccentric relative would react. She was not disappointed.

'Well, you're not what I expected, sirs, I can tell you that much. I had no idea my grandson was mixing with such a top lofty group of gentlemen in Town.' The old lady raised her lorgnette and stared beadily at both men. 'I would say that both of you are a good ten years his senior. What, may I ask, have you in common?'

Eliza almost choked in an effort to hold back her amusement. She saw twin flags of colour appear on Lord Wydale's cheeks and his nostrils flared and knew it was going to be a disaster. To her astonishment Mr Reed placed a light hand on his friend's arm before moving forward and bowing deeply.

'Mrs Dean, you have seen through us in an instant. Mr Fox is but a casual acquaintance, as you have guessed. We frequent the same clubs, that is all. However, when your grandson saw us walking through your pretty town, he greeted us and, as any gentleman in his situation would do, invited us to join him for dinner.'

Eliza released her breath, impressed with the way the extremely tall man had averted an embarrassing contretemps; she waited to see what her grandmother's answer would be.

'Ah! That explains it; anyone would have done the same as you say. But that doesn't explain why you two Corinthians are in

Dedham in the first place.'

'Madam, we are here to meet with Mr Constable, if we can find him. I wish to commission some landscapes of my home. I believe that he is often seen hereabouts.'

Mrs Fox decided her mother had had more than enough attention from the two gentlemen. 'I am acquainted with Mr Constable, sir, and should be delighted to introduce you if he is staying in the vicinity at the moment. However, I don't believe he visits with his parents as often as he used to. He is more likely to be staying at Wivenhoe House, with General Rebow, who is a patron of his.'

'General Rebow, you say? He is my godfather; it's my intention to call on him whilst in Essex. Thank you, madam, your information has been most valuable.'

Eliza waited for Edmund to say something else, to introduce her and Sarah to the visitors, but for some reason he refrained. She guessed it was to protect Sarah from inquisitive eyes, but it seemed almost to be a deliberate insult and she saw the taller man's shock at this omission. There was no reaction to the slight from Lord Wydale. Mr Reed's expression hardened.

Unsure what to do to resolve the situation, she did nothing. She would no doubt steal a moment to explain why her brother had not

46

introduced them and when he understood how things were with Sarah, perhaps he would not view her brother with such dislike. It was vital that Edmund retained Mr Reed's support, for without his intervention they would already be facing eviction.

Eliza heard the connecting doors to the dining room swing open and Ann, one of the parlour maids, curtsied prettily. 'Dinner is served, my lord, ladies and gentlemen. Would you care to step this way?'

Edmund took his mother's arm, as he always did when he was home; Sarah and Eliza moved across to help their grandmother from her seat. This left the two visitors to walk in side by side.

Eliza glanced round the room in surprise. When had her mother found the time to organize all this polishing and to produce the best china and crystal? Beeswax candles stood in regimental rows down the centre of the long table casting a golden glow over the rosewood surface.

Ann was joined by the other parlour maid, Rose, and together they seated Lord Wydale on the left of Edmund's chair and Mr Reed on his right, then her mother was sat centrally, opposite her grandmother. Sarah and she sat at the far end of the table.

Relieved that she was not obliged to make

small talk with either of the men and Sarah was protected from them also, she waited silently for the maids, watched over by Mrs Green, to serve the first course.

Cook had excelled herself and produced an impressive array of dishes. Leek and ham soup was followed by salmon baked in pastry; there was chicken, cabbage and spinach cake, and also Cook's famous port wine sauce to go with a potato pudding. These dishes were handed round, not placed centrally, which made for a more relaxed atmosphere. It also gave everyone a chance to select what they liked and not be left with whatever happened to be placed near them. The second course was turkey with crayfish, braised beef steaks, raised game pie, syllabub and a magnificent raspberry cake.

By the time they had all eaten their fill, and in the gentlemen's case drunk several bottles of claret, the feeling around the table was convivial and even Eliza began to forget the true purpose of their guests appearance in Dedham.

Sarah had been overwhelmed by the occasion and did not have to be reminded to remain quiet. When Mrs Fox rose gracefully to lead the ladies from the dining room, leaving the gentlemen to their port, Eliza began to believe the evening would pass without disaster.

As soon as they were safely in the drawing room and the doors had closed behind them she pulled the bell strap. Jane would be waiting for this signal downstairs and would arrive before the men had finished drinking to collect her charge and whisk her out of harm's way.

'Sarah, you've been such a good girl, but it is well past your bedtime. Do you know it's almost eight o'clock? If you're to have time to play before you retire, you had best go up with Jane right away.'

'It was a lovely meal, Mama. I hope there is some of that raspberry cake left for me tomorrow.'

Mrs Fox smiled, bent and kissed her daughter fondly on the cheek. 'I believe you and Grandmother were the only two who ate any. I'm sure there will be plenty left for you to have at luncheon.'

There was a tap on the door and Jane appeared. 'There you are, darling. Jane is here to take you up. Say your good nights like a good girl and run along.'

Eliza hugged her sister and then Sarah ran across the room, dropping to her knee to kiss her grandmother's leathery cheek before scrambling up and skipping happily down the long room to take the hand of her maid.

'Can I come down and see the foal

tomorrow morning, Liza?'

'You can; I shall wait for you in the breakfast parlour. Goodnight, darling.'

The door had hardly closed behind them, when she heard chairs being pushed back and movement in the dining room. Good heavens! They could hardly have had time to drink even one glass of port. Had something happened to upset them? Eliza moved away to stand in the shadows of the bay window, leaving her mother and grandmother to greet the guests.

The double doors were pushed open and Lord Wydale entered first, his eyes flashing around the room. She saw the disappointment written on his face when he discovered Sarah was no longer there. Her mother saw it also.

'My lord, I must apologize, but my younger daughter Sarah suffers from headaches and has retired.'

From her hiding place Eliza watched the dark-haired man pin a false smile to his face. 'I am desolated to hear that, madam; perhaps I may be permitted to call tomorrow to enquire how she does?'

The words hung in the air unanswered for an uncomfortable moment. Edmund appeared behind Lord Wydale. 'Remember I am to take you across to Wivenhoe Park, my lord, tomorrow morning. And once my sister has a megrim we often don't see her for several days. Perhaps you could call back another time, when she's well?'

Eliza relaxed, for all his youth her brother appeared to have acquired the necessary aplomb to handle difficult situations. If only he had had the sense to stay out of gambling hells, then none of this would be necessary.

Lord Wydale flicked a glance in her direction and found her wanting. As his quarry had flown, he made it clear from his look of boredom that he was ready to take his leave as soon as it was polite to do so.

She watched in horror as his companion smiled warmly at her mother and grandmother and then headed purposefully in her direction. She backed away, hoping he would get the message and rejoin his friend, but he didn't.

'Miss Fox, we have not been formally introduced. Allow me to present myself, I am Fletcher Reed, at your service.'

Eliza dipped in a brief curtsey keeping her head lowered, unwilling to make eye contact. Although this man did not have the good looks of his companion, there was something about him that she found unnerving. Perhaps it was his height; there were not many men she was obliged to look up to.

51

Reluctantly she straightened, slowly raising her head, knowing she could not keep her eyes fixed to the floor indefinitely. She found herself caught by his smoky blue-grey gaze and found it difficult to make the required response.

'I am delighted to make your acquaintance, sir. It was not ill manners on my brother's part that prevented us from being introduced. My sister Sarah is not as other young women: she is blessed with beauty but God did not see fit to give her the intelligence to match.'

As she spoke she watched a look of disbelief and then total stupefaction cross his face. Surely the information that her sister was a simpleton had not caused this?

'I knew it. I believe, Miss Fox, that you owe me an apology.'

'Surely you don't wish me to apologize for Sarah's disability?' Her voice dripped ice.

'Of course not. I am speaking of something else entirely. Miss Fox, I knew when I first saw you this evening that you were familiar to me and I couldn't quite place where we had met. I thought it must be in Town when you had your season a few years ago. However, as soon as you raised your head and looked at me I recognized you as the gentleman on the chestnut gelding who covered us in mud.'

Eliza took an incautious step backward,

forgetting she was not dressed in britches, but in an evening dress and the heel of her slipper snagged in the hem of her gown and she felt herself falling backwards.

Two long arms shot out and, grasping her by the elbows, lifted her from her feet as if she weighed no more than a bag of apples. She was replaced with a decided thud. Flustered by the intimate contact she stammered her thanks.

'Thank you, sir. Without your intervention I should have suffered a nasty fall.'

'I was tempted to allow you to do so, it is no more than you deserve after your cavalier behaviour this morning.'

Eliza busied herself shaking out her gown whilst trying to think of something inoffensive to say. 'If you'd not been skulking about in places that do not concern you I should not have covered you both with mud.' She gulped nervously, that was not what she had intended at all.

His shout of laughter startled her and the rest of the drawing room. She was painfully aware that they were the centre of attention.

'I must apologize for causing you to be discommoded. But you can imagine how I viewed the meeting, coming so soon after being told by my brother that he had lost Grove House in a game of chance to Lord Wydale.'

'Indeed I do, my dear Miss Fox, and covering us with dirt was exactly the right thing to do to smooth the situation over, don't you think?'

She clapped her hands over her mouth, trying to stifle a gurgle of mirth. She glanced up through her lashes and wished she hadn't. He was funning her — he was finding the whole situation as amusing as she was.

Hastily turning her back on the interested spectators watching from the far end of the room, she pretended to gaze out across the invisible park. 'It is no laughing matter, sir, in three months' time we shall all be destitute.' She was aware that he had come to stand beside her; she could feel the warmth from his shoulder as it rested against her arm.

'Listen to me, Miss Fox, I give you my word as a gentleman that you and your family shall not lose your home.'

'Thank you, sir, but I cannot accept your charity. If there is to be a way out of this, it has to come from within the family.'

'You have some funds elsewhere? Money that your brother cannot touch?'

Surprised at his acuteness she risked a glance sideways. 'Yes, sir, that's correct. I have no idea how much, but am hoping it will be enough to at least buy back the small estate my father intended us to retire to when

Edmund came into his majority.'

'And if it isn't enough, what then?'

'Then I shall ask you to shoot Wydale through the heart and remove the obstacle for me.' She smiled, unaware how this simple gesture transformed her face from ordinary to breathtaking.

His throat convulsed and she felt the tension in his body. What had she said to discompose him? The moment was broken by a call from across the room.

'Eliza, my dear, come and play for us. I have just been telling dear Lord Wydale how proficient you are on the pianoforte and he is eager to hear you play.'

Eliza spun, sending a swirl of gold and yellow around her ankles. She saw the hateful man lounging in an armchair, yawn widely and close his eyes. Incensed by his rudeness she was tempted to try and play as Sarah did, hitting the wrong notes as frequently as the right.

However, as always, when her fingers rested on the keys a kind of peace came over her and she lost herself in the music. She played a sonata from beginning to end. She had difficulty hiding her astonishment when both Wydale and Mr Reed began to applaud and congratulate her with every evidence of sincerity. She smiled and bowed her head to acknowledge the praise.

'That's a favourite piece of mine, I am so glad you both enjoyed it.'

Lord Wydale was on his feet, no sign of the indolent and disdainful aristocrat in his dark eyes. 'Bravo, I have never heard anyone play that better. In fact, I can safely say your talent is exceptional.' Eliza saw a gleam in his eyes as he continued smoothly, 'Indeed, if ever the need arose, I believe you could make a living playing in a concert hall.'

Eliza felt as if a bowl of icy water had been tipped over her head; her joy in the moment evaporated. He could not have made his meaning clearer. Under his show of politeness and charm this man was ruthless and intended to take Grove House from them.

Before she could respond intemperately Mr Reed stepped up to her and took her hand, raising it to his mouth in a gesture of such sweetness she forgot her anger.

'You are exceptional in every way, Miss Fox. I shall be several days away, but may I have your permission to call on you tomorrow before we leave for Wivenhoe Park?'

For some reason she found no words to answer him, just nodded shyly, but knew that her eyes told him all he needed to know. He released her and turned briskly to face his hostess.

'We have had a delightful evening and thank you for your generous hospitality, madam.' He turned to address Mrs Dean, but she had fallen asleep in her chair. 'Miss Fox has given me permission to call tomorrow. I doubt if I'll receive a reply from the general before noon. Thank you again. Good night.'

Eliza watched him outstare his friend and saw Wydale capitulate. 'Your servant, madam, Miss Fox. I shall long remember this evening; your graciousness has been so welcoming, that I almost feel as if I'm in my own home.' He deliberately glanced up at her as he spoke. She felt her courage wither. Whatever his friend had said, Lord Wydale would not be deflected from his purpose.

She watched him stroll out followed by his much more agreeable friend. Eliza wondered at this connection to the loathsome lord. Mr Reed was obviously a man of substance. If he intended to contact Constable and commission several landscapes he had more money than they would ever have.

She had met several such gentleman during her one painful season and knew they were always seeking ways to alleviate the boredom of their lives. They had nothing to do with their time but gamble and drink whilst in Town and hunt and shoot when in the country.

Her face set in determination. She would find a way through this, she didn't mind what it took. Jane was waiting for her in her bedchamber.

'Jane, there was no need for you to wait up for me. You know that I'm quite capable of removing my own garments, even one as elaborate as this.'

The young woman didn't smile. 'I had to speak to you, miss, I'm that worried I couldn't sleep until I told you.'

'What is it? Is Sarah unwell?'

'No, it's worse than that. For all she's a child in her head, she has feelings like a woman grown. Miss Sarah has done nothing but talk about 'Lord Wydale this and Lord Wydale that', over and over. She says as she's going to marry him and be his princess.'

'We knew this must come sometime, Jane. Doctor Smith told us that Sarah would have such feelings. It's up to us to keep her safe from that man. He will soon be gone and she will forget she ever met him.'

Eliza hid her disquiet until she was alone. First Edmund had gambled away their home and now a dissolute aristocrat was taking an unhealthy interest in her sister just at the time Sarah was feeling unsettled by her physical maturity.

She rarely allowed herself the luxury of

tears; someone had to keep their emotions under control, and that someone was always her. Tonight, for some reason, she felt more vulnerable. Why had her defences begun to crumble when she needed them most?

6

'Liza, when will it stop raining? When can I go out and see Polly? Why doesn't that nice man come and talk to me?'

'We shall go out and see the foal as soon as it stops raining, Sarah. And why should anybody wish to visit us when the weather is so inclement?' Eliza hoped she was correct in this assumption as the last thing she wanted was for Lord Wydale to strike up a friendship with her sister. She had discussed the matter with her mother over breakfast and they had both agreed to do their best to keep Sarah away if he came to call.

Eliza knew this passion for Wydale would fade as quickly as any other and Sarah would move on to something else, but she was concerned that circumstances might make it almost impossible to keep the two apart.

Edmund joined them in the cosy parlour they used during the day. 'As I was dressing I saw a closed carriage approaching. It's not our visitors from last night — they had a much smarter vehicle — so it must be the lawyer.'

Eliza sprang to her feet, smiling at her

sister's eager expression. 'Sorry, sweetheart, it's not that nice man coming to see you. It's a very boring old man coming to talk to Edmund and me about business matters. Why don't you go upstairs to the nursery and play with your dolls. I promise I shall join you as soon as I've finished down here.'

Sarah frowned, the promise not enough to placate her desire to play princes and princesses with the gentleman who had smiled at her several times during dinner last night.

Edmund recognized the danger signals. 'What if I come up as well? We could play a game of hide and go seek in the attics.'

Sarah clapped her hands. There was nothing she liked better than playing with her older brother and sister and especially in the attics. 'Thank you, Edmund. I shall go upstairs and tell Jane to show me some really good hiding places.'

The girl-woman, her hair once more tumbling down her back, pushed back her chair and ran out of the room ahead of them to find her beloved companion.

'Well done, Edmund. You have saved us from a nasty tantrum. Please excuse us, Mama, I'm hoping this will be the good news we all want.'

Eliza and Edmund had decided to tell their

mother that there might be a small trust fund that could pay off Edmund's gambling debts right away and allow him to return to London. Eliza and Edmund crossed the narrow hall and walked down to the room that faced the gravel-covered carriage sweep. The library and study had been their father's refuge from his wife and mother-in-law.

Eliza seated herself behind the desk forgetting that it was Edmund's place to sit there; she was so used to commanding affairs, she considered it her place as of right. Edmund, an easy-going young man, took no offence, and went to prop himself in the window seat.

Fiddling nervously with the tassels on his Hessian boots, rubbing specks from their shiny surface, he was obviously uneasy. She knew exactly how he felt; her heart was racing and her mouth unpleasantly dry.

Today she had dressed in a dark-green cambric gown which had a high neck and long sleeves. The elegant cut more than made up for its lack of ornamentation. She heard the bell ring loudly and then Rose's voice. She sat and prayed fervently that it might be better news than she expected.

There was a knock on the door and it opened. 'Begging your pardon, sir, miss, Mr Firmin is here to see you.'

A middle-aged gentleman dressed entirely in black, his head a mass of grey curls around a bald centre, smiled at them both, bowing deeply. 'My dear Miss Fox, Mr Fox, in what way can I be of service to you this morning?'

'Thank you for coming to see us so promptly. Please take a seat. There's a matter of extreme urgency we have to discuss.' Briefly Eliza explained the situation and watched the jovial man's expression change to one of alarm. She reached the part about the mysterious fund and he looked at her blankly.

'Trust funds? Funds invested in your name, to access whenever you please? Miss Fox, I have no knowledge of this.'

Eliza flinched. She closed her eyes trying to absorb this latest piece of devastating news.

Edmund burst out, 'My God, we are ruined! I might as well blow my brains out now and save myself the trouble later.'

His overly dramatic exclamation brought Eliza back to her senses. 'Don't be so ridiculous, Edmund. You have responsibilities; you're the head of this household, or will be next March. There is no time for such nonsense. Father told me there was money and there must be some, even if Mr Firmin does not know of its whereabouts.'

The lawyer was wringing his hands, his

face etched deep with concern for his young clients. Eliza stared at him, waiting for him to offer them some advice. None was forthcoming.

'Mr Firmin, think back five years ago, did anything happen at your chambers that might account for this piece of information not being at your fingertips?'

She watched the gentleman's face clear miraculously. 'Five years ago you say, Miss Fox? Of course, that was when my dear father passed away and I was unable to take over the business because my wife was desperately ill with child-bed fever.' He frowned and Eliza held her breath, waiting for him to continue.

'Who dealt with your clients during that period?' Edmund was not so patient.

'It was my cousin, in London. My clerks dealt with the smaller matters, but anything of importance was transferred at once to Lincoln's Inn Fields. That is where this information must be. I really must apologize, sir, madam, it is most remiss of me. I believed that all such information had been transferred to our office as soon as I returned, but for some reason this particular instruction has remained locked away in London.'

He got to his feet and bowed again deeply. 'I shall send a clerk for it as soon as I return, Miss Fox. I shall have the information you require when I return here at the same time tomorrow morning. Pray excuse me, I must return to my office immediately and get things organized.'

Edmund was, by this time, on his feet and not waiting to ring for a parlour maid to show the lawyer out, did the job himself.

Eliza heard them conversing in the corridor as they walked towards the front door. She felt her heart slowly returning to its normal pace; they were safe, at least until tomorrow. She could dream that the money invested somewhere would be enough to pay off Lord Wydale. Until she knew different she would push her darker thoughts away.

Edmund returned, a grin on his face. 'That was a close thing, Liza. For a moment I thought all was lost. I'm sure we'll have the news we want tomorrow; until then I intend to forget all about it, and pretend everything is as it should be. I advise you to do the same. Papa used to say that worrying about a thing won't change it; it merely makes you feel bad.'

She smiled; she could recall her father saying those exact words. 'Come, we had best go upstairs and play that game with Sarah as we promised. The rain is getting heavier thank goodness, so we should not get any more visitors this morning.'

* ★ ★

They played a noisy game in and out of the attics for more than an hour; it was Eliza's turn to count whilst the other two secreted themselves for the umpteenth time. Relieved to have a few moments to herself, she sank on to a nursery chair watching the comforting flicker of the log fire. She heard hurrying footsteps along the uncarpeted hall outside and the door burst open.

'There you are, Miss Fox. Mr Reed has come to call on you and is waiting in the drawing room. Mrs Fox asks that you come down at once and speak to him.'

'Thank you, Jane. I shall be glad to do so. I'm quite worn out playing hide and go seek with Sarah. It's my turn to do the finding, so I'm afraid you must do so instead of me or the two of them will languish behind the trunks until luncheon.'

She felt invigorated, and for a moment was able to forget about their problems as she contemplated a pleasant half an hour in the company of Lord Wydale's most attractive friend. She rushed into her own bedchamber to tidy herself before she descended. She knew exactly where the clothes brushes were placed as she often had need of them. She checked she was free of cobwebs and washed her face to remove the smuts she had acquired whilst crawling around the attics.

Even she could see her eyes were sparkling. It was so long since she had had a gentleman caller, it made her feel like a green girl again. She ran lightly down the stairs, steadying her progress before she entered the drawing room.

She had expected to find her mother and grandmother entertaining the guest but the room was unexpectedly empty of anyone apart from her visitor. She hesitated, not sure if it was indecorous to enter unchaperoned.

He was waiting, standing, apparently relaxed, in the centre of the faded carpet. 'Good morning, Miss Fox. Permit me to say that you look quite delightful in that gown.'

She dipped in a brief curtsey. 'Thank you, sir, and I appreciate your compliment. I had thought to find my mother and grandmother with you. I'm not sure it's correct etiquette for me to entertain you alone.'

'If you leave the door wide open, and we remain standing, I'm sure no one will accuse you of doing anything indelicate.'

She had the distinct impression he was laughing at her. It was so long since she had been in this situation, she had forgotten the rigid rules that governed the *ton*. Smiling up at him she responded to his sally. 'I am sure, sir, my mama cannot object if we move two chairs into the centre of the carpet and sit there. However, I must insist there is a distance of at least a yard between us.'

He bowed solemnly. 'Of course, Miss Fox. An excellent notion. Remain exactly where you are and I shall fetch the chairs at once.'

She watched him stroll across and select two wooden armchairs with matching upholstered seats. She knew each were quite heavy, but he collected them in one hand and placed them exactly as she had specified.

He bowed again, and gestured to the chair nearest the warmth of the hearth. 'Please be seated, Miss Fox. You must remember that a gentleman cannot do so before a lady.'

Trying not to giggle, she folded herself on the chair and, crossing her ankles neatly, she placed her hands on her lap and waited for him to make the next move. He collapsed his long length opposite, crossing his legs and curling his arms around the curved chair back.

'There, I do believe we are ready to exchange commonplaces. Do you have something boring to tell me?' This was too much. Eliza's laughter filled the room, breaking the tension.

'You are impossible, sir. I have never said anything boring in my life. I am a fount of wit and wisdom; you have only to ask my family to discover that I speak nothing but the truth.'

'In which case, Miss Fox, I wait with bated breath to hear what you have to say to me. I am but an ordinary man and have only come to pay you flowery compliments and flirt outrageously.'

The words were spoken lightly, but she saw a glint in his eyes and all desire to laugh left her. For the second time that morning Eliza felt her heart race and her colour fade. She knew she should say something clever, respond with an equally flippant remark.

'Mr Reed, please do not make fun of me. I am not used to making trivial conversation and have never flirted with anyone in my life. I know my own limitations. What is it you want from me? I am what you see, and I will not be made fun of.'

Instantly his face changed and his face became serious. 'My dear Miss Fox, I assure you that I am not making fun of you. You must not sell yourself short. You're a lovely young woman and I own that I am surprised, but delighted, to find you still living at home and not happily married with a family of your own.'

She swallowed. Finding herself unable to think of a suitable reply she answered flippantly. 'Selling myself short, sir, is something I could never do, for I am almost two yards tall in my stockinged feet.'

His shout of laughter startled Rose who was hurrying to the drawing room to enquire if they would like refreshments. The maid appeared in the open doorway, and curtsied.

'Would you be requiring anything, miss?'

Eliza raised an eyebrow at her guest and he shook his head, his lips pressed tight, trying to contain his mirth. 'No, thank you. Mr Reed will not be staying long.'

The girl dipped again and disappeared back down the corridor. Eliza knew the staff would be discussing the unusual circumstance of her entertaining a handsome gentleman caller before said gentleman had even departed the house.

'Good grief! You're an original, Miss Fox.' He wiped his brimming eyes and, ignoring her protests, stood up and moved his chair closer. So close, when he sat down again his knees were almost touching hers.

'My dear, you're a diamond of the first water. I don't know how you could have thought otherwise. I swear I have never seen eyes as beautiful as yours or . . . ' He stopped, and she saw the blood flow into his cheeks and realized he had been going to say something decidedly indelicate. Suddenly she felt liberated, able to say exactly what she thought. Even with her fiancé she had never felt this free.

'Are you, by any chance, referring to my womanly curves, sir? I shall never be mistaken for a country bumpkin when I'm dressed as I should be, that is certain.'

She thought she had gone too far, that she had shocked him by her outspokenness and wished her words unsaid. He ducked his head, hiding his expression and she wondered why he was hunched forward as if in pain.

'Is something wrong, sir? Are you unwell?'

His voice was unexpectedly gruff. 'A touch of gripe, nothing to worry about. Why don't you take a turn around the room and allow me to recover? I shall join you as soon as I'm ready.'

She rose, trying not to let her knees brush his. A hand shot out taking one of hers in a grip that was almost painful. She felt the roughness of his thumb circling and a strange heat rushed to her nether regions making her feel unsettled. She should withdraw immediately, retreat to the safety of the large bay window, but something made her wish to move closer, to feel that hand stroke her in other places.

Shocked rigid by her wanton thoughts, she snatched her hand back and almost ran to hide in the shadow of the semicircular window. She turned to stare out across the drenched terrace and down the vista which her grandfather had created.

He had turned a modest Tudor mansion into a substantial property and had wished to employ the services of Capability Brown, but could not afford his fees. Instead he had copied faithfully from a picture plate and achieved the same result. The formal parterre and ornamental gardens had been ripped up and replaced with lawns and groups of trees; at the far end of this the sparkle of an ornamental lake attracted attention. Even in the pouring rain the view was still beautiful.

She heard the chair move. She didn't know how to react when Mr Reed was close to her saying outrageous things and causing her to behave quite out of character. She sensed him approaching and inhaled his distinctive aroma of lemon and leather. She waited for him to speak, grateful that he stood a good arm's length away.

'I have a similar panorama on my estate. Whoever built this must have employed the services of Capability Brown.'

She relaxed; this was a subject she was happy to converse on indefinitely. Her knowledge of the land was as good as any man's, but for some reason she said something else entirely. 'Forgive me, sir, I have to ask, why do you associate with an evil man? Lord Wydale is not like you. You're a good man, I could tell that as soon as I met you.'

She turned to see his face when he answered. She knew she should not have mentioned her fears, knew she had breached the rules of etiquette. She waited for his reply, expecting it to be a severe set down. Her companion continued to stare morosely out across the landscape then, like her, he swung inwards.

'You're right to ask me. It's a long story; perhaps one day I shall tell you the whole, but let it suffice to say that we shared a miserable childhood together and if it wasn't for his help when I was at school I doubt I should have survived; he showed me how to rise above physical abuse and appear indifferent.'

'And now? You are your own man; I cannot imagine there's anyone or anything that could put you out of countenance. You are the more formidable. Why do you still associate yourself with him? One day he will do something so wicked he will take you down with him.'

She had gone too far; his eyes narrowed and she waited for the rebuke she richly deserved. Then to her surprise his lips curved into a smile; it was the first time he had smiled directly at her. Her heart skipped. She felt unaccountably breathless and unable to look away. She recovered her equilibrium sufficiently to speak.

'Do you feel you have to keep Lord Wydale out of mischief?'

He shook his head. 'No, frankly, it's too late for that. I do my best to protect others from him. I am here to try and undo the wrong he has done to your brother.' Seeing the look of horror on Eliza's face he added hastily, 'Oh, I assure you, he never cheats. He's known to be the best card player in Town. No one of sense will accept his challenge. He deliberately set out to charm your brother and tricked him into playing.'

'I see. I'm hoping I can raise enough money from a trust fund to pay this debt. Have you any idea how much my brother signed away?'

'I have not seen all his vowels, but I believe that they add up to more than thirty thousand guineas.'

This shocking discovery was too much. For the first time in her life she felt her knees buckle and the last thing she remembered was being clasped in the arms of a man she had only known for twenty-four hours, but who had already become something more than a friend.

Fletcher caught Eliza easily, her substantial weight nothing to a man of his size. With a muttered curse he lifted her and turned to scan the room for somewhere suitable to put her down. He strode across the room and placed his unconscious burden on the only piece of furniture that was long enough to accommodate her. He pushed a pillow gently under her head, pausing for a moment at her side, drinking in her features like a man parched in a desert.

Why had he not seen her five years before, when she spent a season in London? He had always disliked his abnormal height and build, feeling clumsy around the dainty Dresden misses that he came across in the drawing rooms of society, and knew that he would have felt as comfortable with her then as he did now.

Lying unconscious on the daybed beside him was a young woman who made him a perfect match. She was statuesque, with eyes the colour of cornflowers and hair like new mown hay. She was intelligent and funny and had no more wish to sit around embroidering useless tapestries than he did.

Glancing hastily over his shoulder to see that they were unobserved, he bent his head and stole a fleeting kiss from the sleeping beauty. Only then did he spring to his feet and yank the bell-strap vigorously. The housekeeper appeared with such alacrity he felt she must have been waiting to receive a summons.

'Miss Fox has swooned. I do not believe she is unwell, but she needs to be attended to. I shall take my leave, I am *de trop*. Please tell Miss Fox I shall call tomorrow to see how she does.'

Without waiting for the startled woman to reply he stepped past and took his hat from the hall-stand and walked briskly down the long narrow hall and out into the pouring rain. It was only as he stood, marooned under the portico that he realized he had left his riding coat behind.

He grinned to himself, he was behaving like a lovesick boy. He turned and, as he did so, the front door swung open and a smiling maid silently handed him the missing garment. Nodding his thanks, he shrugged it on, buttoning it up around his neck against the weather. Jamming on his beaver he strode off into the rain to find his mount, which no doubt had been eating his head off in a warm stable somewhere at the rear of the building. He cantered the mile back into the village of Dedham and clattered through the archway at the Sun Inn. Immediately an ostler appeared at his side.

'A rum old day, sir. I'll take your horse, shall I? You'll be wanting to get inside and dry off.'

Fletcher dismounted and tossing the toothless old man a coin ran inside the ancient building. In the smoky beamed hall he unbuttoned his coat and shook it vigorously before tossing it over his arm. The landlady appeared from the snug.

'Ah! Mr Reed, sir. His lordship was enquiring after you. He's in his parlour breaking his fast and I believe he wishes to speak to you on a matter of some urgency.'

Fletcher looked down at the dripping coat over his arm and the landlady bustled forward. 'Here, sir, let me take that, I'll get it dried for you in no time. I'll put the coat back in your chamber as soon as it's fit to be worn.' She nodded in the direction of the window. 'But I doubt if you're going outside again this morning, not in this weather.'

Ignoring her chatter he smiled his thanks and headed for the stairs. He and Wydale had been given the best rooms in the place: he had a bedchamber and parlour at the rear of the building, overlooking the stable yard and Wydale had a matching pair overlooking the busy main street.

Outside Lord Wydale's room he paused, a strange feeling of reluctance coming over him. He could recall exactly his conversation with Miss Fox and her damning condemnation of the man who called him friend. She was quite correct. It was long past time to sever the connection and leave the man to go to perdition anyway he chose. He knocked, but without waiting for an answer pushed open the door.

'Reed, when are we leaving for Wivenhoe Park? It's damned boring cooped up in here in the rain.'

'I shall send a note straightaway. I have arranged to call in at Grove House to see Miss Fox tomorrow; I cannot depart before then.'

Wydale shrugged. 'So I must spend a further day in this dismal place? I swear that I cannot see what that artist fellow, Constable, sees in the countryside. Dedham is a dreary hole and if I didn't have property here I should never visit again.'

Fletcher gritted his teeth, biting back his angry retort. How could he ever have seen this man as acceptable? However, he must keep up the pretence until he had persuaded Wydale to sell him the vowels. It would not do to cause offence until he had achieved his objective.

'I'm going to change my clothes, then shall send my groom over to Wivenhoe. I am obligated to remain until tomorrow, but there's no reason why you cannot go as soon as I hear from General Rebow. You have a closed carriage so the rain should not bother you.'

'Aren't you forgetting the delectable Miss Fox?' Wydale sneered.

'As I have said, Wydale, I shall ride over on my own tomorrow. It is merely a courtesy visit, Miss Fox was unwell when I called earlier this morning.'

Without waiting for an answer Fletcher turned on his heel and marched out before he punched the man lolling in his chair, his dark hair in fashionable disarray and his white teeth gleaming in a knowing smirk.

He wrote his note to General Rebow but included a request that the Fox family be invited also. He doubted if Eliza had the opportunity to attend many social functions outside her home. Smiling, he sanded the paper and folded it neatly, sealing it with a blob of red wax.

He had no intention of commissioning any artist to paint landscapes of his estate. However, spending an evening in the company of Miss Fox was something he was eagerly anticipating.

7

The smell of burning feathers roused Eliza. She opened her eyes to see her mother's face bending over her, of Mr Reed there was no sign. She realized she was stretched out full-length upon the *chaise-longue* which stood at the far end of the drawing room under a row of family portraits.

'My dear, whatever is the matter? I have sent for Dr Smith and he will be here directly. I do hope you are not sickening for the fever; I have heard that there is some in the next village.'

Wearily Eliza pushed herself upright, swinging her legs down to the ground as she did so. 'I'm fine, Mama. It was shock, nothing more.'

Her mother stared at her as if she had just emerged from Bedlam. 'Shock? Good heavens, child, what did Mr Reed do to you? Shall I have Edmund call him out?'

This ridiculous suggestion did much to restore Eliza's sang froid. 'No, Mr Reed is a gentleman; it was nothing that *he* did upset me. I think it's time that I told you the whole truth, Mama. You had better sit down, I'm certain the shock of what I'm about to say might make you swoon as well.'

She waited for her parent to draw up the same curved backed chair she had used earlier and then began her sorry tale. She left nothing out, told Mrs Fox the whole, including the astronomical amount of vowels Edmund had so foolishly signed and the slight chance that there was enough to save them invested in the funds.

'It's no wonder, my dear, that you fainted. How could you have kept this from me? The burden is for all of us to share. If we're to remove from Grove House in a matter of weeks, arrangements have to be made, staff have to be told. You cannot expect things like this to be arranged at short notice.'

Eliza could hardly believe what she was hearing. She had expected her mother to wail and wring her hands, but she had misjudged her. 'I apologize, Mama. I thought to save you, Grandmamma and Sarah from the worst until I actually knew how bad things were. I realize now that whatever Papa invested for me, it will never cover the amount that we owe that hateful man.'

'Hockley House, I suppose that will have gone as well?' Eliza nodded sadly. 'Then I must write at once to your Uncle Benjy. You have never met him; he is two years my senior and never married. He lives in the home in which I grew up, a comfortable estate in a village near St Albans. He will take us all; indeed he has asked me several times since your father died to join him at Cranston and be his housekeeper. It's not as comfortable nor nearly as pretty as Grove House, but it is large enough to accommodate us.

'Why have you never mentioned this uncle before? He has never visited or to my certain knowledge, sent gifts for our name days or at Christmas. How can you be sure, after so long, that he will wish to have his privacy invaded?'

Her mother smiled. 'He's not an easy man to live with. If I am honest, he has a miserly turn of mind. Living there, on his charity will not be pleasant, but at least we shall have a roof over our heads.' Mrs Fox stood up, her normal languid style forgotten.

'Edmund is his heir, you know. Whatever happens here, he will not be penniless. When your uncle dies your brother can restore Cranston to its former glory and make it a happy place once more.'

Eliza was determined not to cavil at this opportunity that her mother had produced from nowhere. She felt a shiver of disquiet at the thought of living with someone where every penny was counted and every mouthful watched. Poor Sarah; she would shrivel under such an austere regime.

'Shall you write to Uncle Benjy, then, Mama? We do not wish to turn up on his doorstep, like gypsies, unannounced?'

'Of course I shall write to him, Eliza. However, I think you were right not to tell Grandmamma or Sarah about this. Also, until we are certain what Wydale wishes to do regarding the staff, we shall not worry them. But we must tell Jane, Marie Baptiste and my mother's maid, Betty. I suppose that Edmund will require to take Denver with him, but the rest will have to stay here, or be dismissed, and it's better that they do not know this until we're certain.'

Eliza agreed. 'My money can be used to provide pensions for the staff, that at least will solve *that* problem. I could not bear to think of our family retainers being cast aside when they are too old to find employment elsewhere. And neither do I wish them to work for Lord Wydale. They would hate it and he would not appreciate their worth.'

'I should keep some money by, my dear. It will be pleasant for us to provide ourselves with a few luxuries and the occasional new gown; you can be certain that my brother will not wish to do so.'

'Mama, can I ask you not to say anything,

or send that letter to my uncle, until we are sure how things stand financially? It still might be possible to pay off sufficient of the debt to enable us to move to Hockley House.'

'Very well, my dear. I shall leave the matter as it is for the moment. You have a wise head on young shoulders, and you have steered us through bad times before.' Her mother rose, her face more animated than it had been since Papa died. 'By the way, Mr Reed said he would call tomorrow morning to see how you are.'

Her mother smiled archly. 'Perhaps all might yet be well? I do believe that gentleman is enamoured of you. He was white as a sheet when he called us in to attend to you.'

Eliza felt a flicker of something warm rush through her. 'Nonsense. Good heavens! We only met yesterday. How could he possibly have formed an attachment in so short a time?'

Even as she spoke the words she remembered how dear Dickon had seen her sitting, like an extremely large wallflower at Almack's, and known that she was the one he had been looking for. Was it possible that Mr Reed had also seen something in her that she could not see herself?

'I'm going upstairs to change into my work clothes, Mama. I need to get out of the house; a brisk gallop around the estate will clear my head of cobwebs.'

Perhaps she would meet Lord Wydale and be able to cover him with mud a second time. She felt a surge of anticipation as she considered the remote possibility that Mr Reed would also be riding and that their paths might inadvertently cross.

She paused at the door. 'Oh dear, what about that Dr Smith? He will be arriving here expecting to find me unconscious and needing his attentions.'

Before she received her answer she heard the clatter of booted feet on the stairs and Edmund arrived, Sarah not far behind him.

'Thank God. Jane said you had taken poorly. What happened? I must say you look remarkably sprightly now.'

Eliza flushed, reluctant to admit her weakness. Mrs Fox answered for her.

'Your sister swooned. She heard some shocking news, but is fully recovered now and I shall send another messenger to tell Dr Smith he's no longer required.'

'Shocking news?' Edmund paled as he was fixed by his mother's basilisk stare. Eliza saw him swallow nervously, and took pity on him.

'Edmund, Mama knows it all and has come up with an excellent solution. We shall not talk about it now, but I'm sure it will be explained to you later. I'm going upstairs to change into my work clothes and am going riding. Do you wish to come with me?'

Edmund glanced through the drawing room to the bay windows which were running with water. 'Are you mad? It's tipping down out there; you will be drowned in an instant. Far better to stay in and play spillikins with Sarah.'

Eliza sighed, she had not realized the rain had worsened. It would indeed be foolish to venture outside. 'Very well, I shall remain indoors until the rain lessens.' She smiled at Sarah whom she could see staring anxiously from face to face wondering what had upset the adults in her life. 'It's all right, darling, there's nothing wrong. Shall we go into the back parlour and draw some pictures?'

'I should like that, Liza. I'm quite puffed out with playing hide and go seek upstairs. Poor Jane says she will need to have a lie down.' Chatting happily she led the way into the small room on the other side of the house and Eliza followed her. She glanced back and saw her mother and Edmund enter the library. She smiled; it would do him no harm to receive a bear-garden jaw. It was time he faced his responsibilities and time that she relinquished hers.

She stopped, amazed at herself for thinking

such a thing. She had been dreading the time when she would be obliged to hand over the running of the estate to her brother believing that she would have no life worth living but that of a dutiful daughter, granddaughter and older sister. Even the prospect of running Hockley House did not fill her with excitement.

How could she have suffered such a *volte face* in less than twenty-four hours? The image of a huge bear-like man, with smoky-blue eyes and a smile that turned her insides over, slid into her mind.

It seemed that after five long empty years she had finally met a kindred spirit, a man who could perhaps replace the void that Dickon's death had left in her life.

Sarah tugged at her hand impatiently. 'Liza, you're not listening to me. Where are the chalks and slate, I can't find them anywhere?'

The drawing things were soon unearthed in the massive oak sideboard and she was content to while away the morning helping Sarah draw pictures, whilst her mind drifted happily over interesting possibilities.

★ ★ ★

The following day her grandmother was given Sarah to entertain whilst Edmund, Mrs Fox and Eliza waited impatiently in the library for the arrival of Mr Firmin.

'I do hope his clerk was able to return from Town in time, Mama. The roads must have been awash after the rain we had yesterday.'

Edmund was staring morosely out of the window. Since his conversation with his mother the previous day he seemed to have sobered and accepted responsibility for what he'd done. He spoke no more of suicide, or running away to sea, but had spent two hours writing notes in the library of possible ways of raising money. 'It's sunny enough now, Liza. The roads would have dried out by this morning. I'm sure he will have the news we want.'

They did not have long to wait before there was the distinct sound of a carriage trundling down the drive.

'It is strange, Mama, that Papa never discussed the matter with you. Are you sure he never told you about this investment he made on my behalf?'

'No, my dear. At least we can be sure he will not have put it in slaves. However much money was to be made he never invested anything in that repugnant trade.'

This time Eliza sat with her mother to one side of the desk and Edmund took his rightful place. She smiled slightly, thinking how much had changed and in such a short time. Less than three days before she had been galloping around the place dressed as a man and Grove House had been safe. Now, she had no wish to wear anything but female attire and Wydale almost had possession of their precious home. All that stood between them and eviction was Mr Firmin and whatever his clerk had discovered in London.

'Edmund, what do you know of Mr Reed? Is he wealthy?'

'I've no idea, Liza. I imagine he has money; he couldn't dress as he does or ride such a horse. I believe he has a house in Grosvenor Square. But he cannot be a man of real substance, or why would he fraternize with such as Wydale.'

Her brother was no doubt correct. Then she remembered something he had said about his family estate, when he had been pretending to be seeking out John Constable the artist. He had mentioned the family home, Longshaw, she thought he had called it, but had also mentioned having an estate of his own.

Her thoughts were interrupted as the lawyer was announced. He began without preamble. 'Good morning to you all. I have the documents you require. The names of the companies inscribed thereon are very hopeful, very promising indeed.' He walked across and placed the box on the desk.

Eliza waited for Edmund to move then remembered that these papers were addressed to her, so it was up to her to open them. She got up and, with shaking hands, removed the first of the five papers. She recognized the name of a manufacturing company. She knew this was making its owners and shareholders rich beyond belief. She untied the red ribbon and flattened the paper.

Edmund leant forward eagerly. 'What does it say, Liza? Tell us at once.'

'Good heavens! It seems I hold five hundred shares in this company. Mr Firmin, how much are they worth, do you know?'

The elderly gentleman rubbed his hands and beamed. 'My dear, Miss Fox, those shares are worth at least ten pounds apiece; that is over five thousand pounds that you're holding.'

'Mama, come and open one of these, Edmund you take another. I do believe we might have the answer to our prayers right here in this box.'

Twenty minutes later they were sitting in the drawing room sipping coffee and eating slices of Cook's delicious plum cake. It was as if a weight had been lifted from her shoulders and even Mr Firmin was included in the celebration.

'I can hardly believe it. Your father was a clever man, Miss Fox. Five years ago none of these companies was more than starting out, so he would have bought the shares cheaply. He was always an astute businessman and he has left you a tidy legacy.'

'I do not see why he would believe I should disapprove of his investments.'

For once Edmund was able to demonstrate he was more worldly than she.

'Child labour, Liza. They make their money by employing children and women on pathetic wages. I believe they also take children from the poorhouse and make them work a so-called apprenticeship.'

'I see. I knew that children were employed in factories, but there are many Members of Parliament who are against this practice, and I'm sure it will be banned eventually.' Eliza could hardly refuse to sell her shares just because the profit was made by exploiting women and children. A rough estimate of the value of the shares was almost £25,000. Not quite enough, but perhaps Lord Wydale could be persuaded to wait for the rest until the next quarter's rents came in.

The lawyer replaced his porcelain cup carefully on the side table. 'Forgive me, ladies, Mr Fox, I must take my leave. As I am to sell these shares for you I must go to

91

London and put matters in hand. How soon do you require the funds, Miss Fox?' He had not been told the whole, but he had guessed the urgency of the matter.

'It is a debt of honour that we have to pay and we have three months to find the money. Will you be able to sell by then?'

'Yes, Miss Fox. The shares will be snapped up as soon as they're available. I shall have the money to you long before the deadline, never fear.'

Edmund rose and shook the older man's hand vigorously. 'Sir, you're a good friend to this family. I hope we can rely on your discretion in this matter?' The older man looked offended and Edmund realized his mistake. 'I do apologize, sir, I'm unused to dealing with such matters. Miss Fox has had to take control of things, but all that is to change today. I intend to stay at home and learn how to run the estates myself.'

Mr Firmin bowed. 'I'm glad you are, sir. You are very like your father and I am certain that Grove House will not suffer in your hands.' The door closed behind him and the three remaining occupants smiled, delighted everything had turned out so well.

'What time did Mr Reed say he would be coming, Mama?'

'He didn't specify a time, my dear. But,

unlike when one's in Town, I'm sure he won't leave his morning call until this afternoon.' Mrs Fox stood up. 'I had better go and see what Grandmamma is doing. She must feel sadly neglected this morning.'

'I am going upstairs to change into my new riding habit. When Mr Reed arrives could you direct him down to the lake? I intend to ride there today.'

Eliza was obliged to struggle out of her day dress and into her riding habit without assistance. Eventually she had all the pieces in place and the jaunty military-style cap firmly pinned to her head. The blue of the closely fitting jacket complemented her eyes and the gold buttons relieved the plainness of the outfit.

She had never worn this habit and neither had she ridden her father's gelding side saddle. Should she change back into her britches? She shook her head; since she had met Mr Reed she had no desire to dress like a farmer. She smiled to herself, as she hurried back down the stairs, at the thought that she would rather risk a tumble than ride astride.

8

Eliza was so unused to riding sidesaddle she found it hard to maintain her balance on the restless chestnut gelding. This horse was also unfamiliar with having his rider sitting sideways and not astride. She was beginning to fear she had made a grave error of judgement in insisting that Fred Smith, the coachman, had saddled this particular horse.

Maybe it would have been better, as he had tactfully suggested, to have taken the quiet cob that Sarah rode. Several times the chestnut shied and bucked and twice Sarah lost her stirrup and only by grabbing a handful of his wiry mane did she manage to remain aloft.

Perhaps if she gave him his head, allowed him a long gallop, he would settle. She leant forward and patted his sweating neck, feeling the heat through her leather gloves.

'Calm down, Sultan, you will have me off in a moment and I'm sure you do not wish to do that. We are the best of friends, aren't we, old fellow?' She watched the horse's ears flick back and forth as if he understood her ramblings. The soothing words appeared to work and her mount relaxed and stopped fighting her.

'You *are* a good boy. Now, if you're ready shall we have a wonderful gallop down the avenue and around the lake?' She shortened her reins and settled more firmly in the saddle; her horse needed no further encouragement. Stretching his neck and lengthening his stride he was soon flying down the turf, the wind whipping tears from her eyes and the trees on either side a green blur.

She had almost reached the lake when she felt a change in her horse's pace, and an added tension in his muscles. What was it now? She glanced over her shoulder and her mouth curved in a smile of welcome. Thundering behind her on a magnificent black stallion was Mr Reed. He returned her greeting and urged his mount faster, obviously hoping to overtake.

She could not allow this to happen, Sultan was past his prime, but he still hated to be bested. She crouched low and shouted encouragement. However hard she urged him the stallion was not left behind. Slowly she saw his nose appear at her foot, then his head, and then the horse and man were beside her, matching her stride for stride. Laughing, she admitted defeat and sitting back in the saddle, exerted a slight pressure on the bit.

The old chestnut was ready to slow down, he, like her, had met his match. Flank to flank the horses dropped back into an extended canter and finally to a walk.

'My word, Miss Fox, I knew you could ride astride as good as any man I know, but even sidesaddle you are incomparable.'

Eliza felt her smile reaching from ear to ear at his praise. 'I was well taught, sir, we all were. My father was famous in the neighbourhood for his horsemanship.'

The two horses walked side by side happy to amble along and recover from their wild gallop. This gave the riders the opportunity to confer more intimately.

'Miss Fox, I'm glad to see you fully recovered from your swoon of yesterday.'

She had the grace to blush. 'I'm in rude health, as you can see, Mr Reed. And I have had most amazing news this morning. My lawyer brought the documents I was waiting for and it appears that I own around twenty-five thousand pounds' worth of shares in various manufactories. He is at this very moment on his way to London to arrange their sale.'

'Shall we dismount, Miss Fox? There are matters I wish to discuss with you and it is hard to do so when one cannot speak directly.'

Laughing, she agreed. 'You see, just over there, there's a grand folly? It has seats inside and at the rear there is somewhere to tether the horses. Often a groom leaves water and fodder, but it's so long since I have been down here, I'm not sure if that's the case today.'

They urged the horses into a trot and soon arrived at the building that looked like a Greek temple from a distance, the marble walls reflecting pink ripples in the surface of the water.

Eliza barely had time to rein in before her companion vaulted from his horse and tossing the reins over the animal's ears stepped round and lifted her from the saddle. Her heart skittered and her pulse raced. She felt his warm gloved hands around her waist as he held her close to his chest for considerably longer than was necessary.

His mouth curved as her feet were placed on the ground. 'I don't suppose your animal will stand if you toss his reins over his head?'

She shook her head. 'No, I'm certain he will not; in fact I'm sure he would take himself home.'

Eliza reached up and taking hold of her chestnut gelding led him round to the rear of the building and, as she had predicted, warm stalls were waiting. Quickly she tied Sultan to a metal ring and loosened his girth a few holes.

Mr Reed attached the rope to his horse's bridle and ran his hand down its neck. 'They are cool enough to leave, I doubt they'll come to any harm standing about whilst we talk.'

Eliza led the way round to the front of the building and up the ornate marble staircase and into the glazed room.

'I know what you're thinking, sir, this is ridiculous architecture. I can honestly say it's the only folly of any sort in which my father was involved. It was my mother's idea; she had seen a picture of something similar and wanted one exactly the same.'

He chuckled. 'It's fortunate, my dear, that it's so far away from the house it's barely discernible. The lake holds the eye; this marble monstrosity is but a shimmering shape in the background.'

Politely he opened the door and waited for her to enter. It did not occur to her to protest that they were going to be closeted alone together totally unchaperoned. The time for such niceties had passed: she knew she was safe with him.

Inside the building were marble benches on which cushions had been placed. She walked over and looking about sat down. She carefully peeled off her gloves and removed the pins from her hat. Eliza was aware that as she did so he was watching her every move with an undue amount of interest. Flustered she dropped a pin.

'Leave it, Miss Fox. If you're quite finished fiddling about I wish to tell you something. I am on my way to visit General Rebow at Wivenhoe Park and I have left an invitation for you and your family to attend an informal supper and dance tomorrow evening. You will come, won't you?'

Eliza was unsure. 'I am not used to attending such functions any more. Shall there be dancing? I hate dancing; it is most lowering being obliged to stare at the top of a man's head for minutes on end.'

'Don't be a goose, my dear Miss Fox, you shall be dancing with me and I defy you to look at the top of my head without the use of a large box.'

It was some time before her giggling was under control. 'Is that why you wished to come in here? Could you not have mentioned this as we rode?' Looking up she saw something so powerful reflected in his eyes she was almost afraid. He had obviously more than conversation on his mind. She knew she should be outraged, but instead she tilted her head to receive his kiss.

His firm lips covered hers and she felt her

bones soften. Her lips parted of their own volition. Never had she felt this way, not even when Dickon had kissed her. She felt strange, restless and overheated, and wanted to press herself closer. He responded by crushing her against his chest.

Several delightful minutes later he released her and, stepping away with a rueful smile, murmured softly, 'I have just treated you without respect. Only betrothed couples are permitted to exchange such kisses.' He cleared his throat and turned to her, his face sincere.

'I know it is far too quick, but as soon as I saw you two days ago I knew I had found the woman I have been searching for all my life. I thank God that a tragedy prevented you from marrying your captain. Do you wish me to go down on one knee and propose, or may I ask you to do me the honour of being my wife from here?'

His eyes were laughing, but she could feel in spite of his jesting that he was tense, not sure how she would reply.

'Thank you, Mr Reed, you have no need to kneel at my feet. I am delighted to accept your kind offer.' She saw the relief flash across his face. How could such a man as this have fallen so quickly in love with a plain Jane like her? 'However, sir, there are certain things you need to know before our betrothal can be made official.'

She saw the shock cross his face and schooled her features to remain stern, not wishing him to know that she was joking. 'I require any man that I marry to be able to spread a ten-acre field with manure within a day; to plant a field of turnips on the next, and repair three thatched roofs and two chimneys on the third.'

Before she could move he closed the distance between them and gathered her back into his arms. 'You are a nonsensical baggage, my darling, and I'm going to love every moment I spend in your company.'

Eliza sighed with pleasure. 'But, you have not answered me, sir. I have asked you a question, I must have satisfaction on all counts if I am to marry you.'

His answer was more growl than speech. 'Sweetheart, I assure you that I shall satisfy you, and I'm not referring to agriculture.' She heard him clear his throat. 'My given name is Fletcher, from now on you shall be Eliza to me. I imagine that after what has taken place between us, it's permissible for us to use given names.'

'As we have only known each other two days, I think it might be wise not to mention this arrangement until we have been acquainted

a little longer — which means we must pre-
serve the formalities as well.'

For answer he scooped her up and headed
back to the bench settling her comfortably on
his lap. 'If you insist, my love, but I promise
you I am an impatient man. Once I have
made up my mind on a matter I do not take
kindly to delay.'

'A June wedding would be most acceptable, sir. That is scarcely two months away.'

'Excellent. When am I to be permitted to
speak to your family?'

'Let me think. If we spend tomorrow
evening in each other's company and then
you come here to us again, that should be
enough to satisfy the proprieties. Speak to
Mama after that.'

They sealed their agreement with a further
blissful few minutes. Then, to her astonishment and dismay, she found herself placed
firmly back on to the cushions. Fletcher
retreated to stare out across the lake, his back
firmly to her.

'Whatever is wrong? Have I offended you
in some way?'

'No, my darling, you have not.'

Delighted, she jumped to her feet and was
preparing to run towards him. He gestured
with one arm. 'No, stay where you are for the
moment. I need to recover.' Still with his back

to her, he said, his voice affectionate, 'I believe there is still a lot you need to know about what happens between a man and woman when they're in love. Were you not on intimate terms with your fiancé?'

Startled, Eliza shook her head. 'Whatever can you mean? Intimate terms? Of course we were not; he was an absolute gentleman. I do not believe we kissed more than three times and never in the way we have just done.'

'That explains it, my darling. Certain things happen to a man when he — how shall I put it — finds a woman desirable.' Curious she crept closer, wishing to know exactly what he was referring to. He continued in a conversational tone, 'Have you never seen animals mate?'

She froze. Surely he could not mean that? She had indeed seen Princess, eleven months ago, being served by a stallion. She clutched her chest in shock. She sensed he had turned towards her but didn't know where to look, certain she would glance down at his unmentionables, and nervous at what she might see there.

'Darling girl, I see you understand to what I'm referring. The same thing happens to all species. Creation could not take place without it.'

Feeling decidedly uncomfortable at the

indelicate turn of the conversation, but pleased Fletcher had explained matters to her, she looked at him shyly. 'I apologize for causing you discomfort. I shall keep my distance in future.'

'I shall have something to say if you do! I intend to kiss you at every opportunity, and I shall have no argument on that score.'

'Shall we sit down again? There's something I wish to ask you about — your friend Lord Wydale. Do you think he would take less than we owe? We don't have the whole amount just now.'

'I have not the slightest notion, sweetheart, but the money is no longer an issue. As your unofficial fiancé, I shall take care of everything.'

He raised her hand to his mouth and kissed each finger tenderly. She forgot what she had asked as she swayed back into his arms.

It was a considerable while later when he finally released her. Too breathless to speak she rested her head against his chest listening to the pounding of his heart. She could hardly believe that it was she who caused this passion. Finally she had found someone to share her life with. She would never be lonely again. And maybe in a year or so she would be holding a baby in her arms. Eliza realized she too had fallen in love in less than three days.

'All my life, my love, I have felt awkward, as if I was missing something, and then three days ago I met you and knew I had found the other half of myself. Apart, we were two lonely people, together, we make the perfect match.'

Eliza rested her head on his shoulder. 'I know exactly what you mean, Mr . . . err . . . Fletcher. I've always felt awkward in company too; I've never quite understood what was going on or felt that I could join in. I prefer to be out of doors, or busy doing something useful.'

His arms tightened sending another thrill of excitement around her already overheated body. 'Also, my love, it's a great relief to be able to a kiss a woman without being obliged to bend my knees.'

She giggled at his outrageous statement. 'It is a great relief to me also, my dear, that I am not obliged to bend mine when kissing you.'

At his delighted chuckle, she turned her head to smile at him and saw love shining in his eyes. 'I suppose we had better make our way back to the house and try and pretend that nothing out of the ordinary has happened.'

9

The expected invitation from Wivenhoe Park arrived later that evening. Eliza had already informed her mother and Edmund and they were eagerly anticipating attending the informal supper party and dance.

'I have written that we are delighted to accept General Rebow's request for our company tomorrow night,' Mrs Fox told Eliza, when they met for afternoon tea. 'It's so kind of Lord Wydale and Mr Reed to think of us. I cannot remember the last time I attended such an occasion.'

'Well, I don't believe we have ever been invited to quite such a grand event. I'm so glad you persuaded me to refurbish my wardrobe in the latest fashions. I would hate to look a country dowd in such illustrious company.'

Her mother understood her perfectly. 'We should both look quite the thing, I'm sure, my dear. It is a great shame your hair is so short, but I believe wearing it cropped is also all the rage.'

'What time do we need to set off if we are to reach Wivenhoe by eight o'clock?'

'I have no idea, Eliza, but I'm sure that Edmund will know exactly. He's forever riding to Colchester and that is much further.' Her mother pursed her mouth in thought. 'At least I think it is. Where is Edmund, have you any idea?'

Eliza shook her head, she hadn't spoken to her brother since she had met him on his way out just after breakfast. 'We can ask him at dinner tonight. I shall go now and arrange for the carriage to be ready tomorrow afternoon.'

★ ★ ★

The entire family gathered in the drawing room after dinner. Eliza turned to her brother as he flopped down beside her on the well-worn sofa.

'Edmund, at what time do we need to leave for the party tomorrow?'

'The roads are dry so it shouldn't take us more than an hour to get to Wivenhoe Park even in the dark. Of course, if it rains it will take considerably longer.'

Sarah had heard the word party and scrambled up from her game of spillikins. 'I want to come too. I never go to parties, I want to wear a pretty dress and be a princess.'

'Please do not be tiresome, Sarah, you know you do not go to grown-up parties.'

Mrs Fox frowned at her daughter who scowled.

'Perhaps we could have an informal supper party and dance here in a few days' time? Obviously we would need to invite our nearest neighbours as well as Edmund's London friends.'

'That is an excellent notion, Eliza. There, Sarah, it's quite permissible for you to attend a party in your own home, but you will have to promise to behave yourself and to retire when you're told to.'

''Course I will, Mama. I shall be ever so good and Jane can look after me like she always does.'

The matter being settled to everyone's satisfaction Sarah went happily to bed leaving Eliza and her mother to begin the task of compiling a list of suitable guests for their own soirée. Mrs Dean had stomped off to bed declaring that she had no intention of attending a party at her time of life and would have a tray in her room on the night in question.

'Do you think Mr Reed and Lord Wydale will still be in the vicinity next week, Eliza? There's no point in holding this event if they are not able to attend.'

'Mr Reed will be obliged to stay a few days with his godfather at Wivenhoe Park and I assume that Lord Wydale will remain with him. If we make the date, let me see, next Friday, I believe that will give everyone sufficient notice.'

'Five days? Yes, that will be ideal. I shall ask Miss Browning and her sister to attend and then they can play for the dancing. I should hate you to be forced to sit out at the pianoforte all evening, Eliza.'

'Thank you, Mama. It's a kind thought, but I should much prefer not to be obliged to stand up in a country set.' Her eyes shone at the thought of the new dance that was sweeping the ballrooms of the country. 'However, I should certainly like to waltz.' She did not add with whom she wished to dance, there was no need.

★ ★ ★

Wydale and Fletcher decided to ride from Dedham to Wivenhoe leaving their menservants to follow with their baggage in the travelling carriage. On the journey Fletcher made it quite clear to his lordship that no mention was to be made about the money he was owed by Edmund Fox.

He had decided not to discuss the fact that Eliza now had most of the funds needed to pay off the debt. Although they were only unofficially betrothed he considered it was his responsibility to take care of his new family. Wydale would know, as soon as the engagement was announced, that he would have no choice but to accept payment. For some reason he suspected that Wydale would far prefer to ruin the family.

Fletcher already knew that Wivenhoe Park had a dozen members in its house party. The season was still in full swing, but many of the *ton* preferred not to spend the whole time in Town. A few days away at a country house made a welcome break from the noise and smoke of London.

However, he had been horrified to discover John Constable was also in residence. The artist was painting a series of commissions for the general and it seemed was often there. He had no choice but to approach the man. Mrs Fox would be bound to mention when she met him that he was intending to ask him to paint Hendon Manor. He was thankful to discover that Constable had no time in his busy schedule this year, but agreed to contact him at a later date.

He had already been obliged to hide from two predatory matrons with marriageable daughters in tow. He had scarcely set foot in the door the previous day before he was pounced upon with glee. He grimaced at the thought of enduring several more days playing cat and mouse in this manner.

He glanced at the tall clock in the drawing room to see it was almost a quarter to eight. Dinner was over and the resident guests would soon be filling the reception rooms; then the coaches and carriages would start to arrive. He bowed and smiled and nodded when required but kept his gaze fixed firmly on the hall.

The clock struck the hour and the procession of local aristocracy and landowners made their way past the general and his wife and through into the spacious drawing room to join those already enjoying a string quartet and liberally flowing champagne.

He saw Eliza before she saw him. Edmund was escorting his mother and she was walking one pace behind. His breath constricted and he felt an uncomfortable tightness in his closely fitting evening trousers. She was so beautiful — and she was his.

Tonight she was wearing an emerald-green gown with a gauze overdress that sparkled in the candlelight. It was cut square across her magnificent bosom, the bodice covered with the same sparkling material. He was not *au fait* with the latest trends in feminine fashions, but even he knew she looked an incomparable.

Her height allowed her to look over the assembled crowd and meet his eyes. The smile she gave him made his head spin. He was not the only one to notice her arrival. A buzz of appreciation and interest ran round the room. Everyone wanted to know the identity of the beautiful fair-haired young woman.

He shouldered his way through the milling guests and arrived at her side possessively slipping her arm through his — he intended to make sure that every male present knew Eliza belonged to him.

'Fletcher, I'm so glad you're here to take me in. This is worse than going to Almack's as a debutante. I cannot tell you how nervous I'm feeling.'

He drew her closer before answering. 'You look *ravissante*, my love. There is no one here your equal in looks or intelligence.' He smiled at her incredulous expression. 'I promise I am speaking the truth. Look around you, sweetheart, and you shall see a dozen gentlemen longing to be introduced.'

She did as he suggested and he saw the colour surge into her cheeks. 'People are staring at us. I hate it. I think I shall go home again.'

'You shall do no such thing. I intend to spend the entire evening at your side. I can assure you no one will embarrass you.'

He felt the rigidity of her arm slowly dissipate. 'I'm sure they won't dare to even speak to me, Fletcher, if you are by my side with that ferocious scowl on your face.'

They were still laughing when they reached the head of the queue and the introductions were made. 'You are very welcome, my dear Miss Fox,' General Rebow boomed. 'I cannot imagine how such a lovely young lady has been allowed to hide away in Dedham for so long.'

Eliza curtsied gracefully and made a suitably demure reply, but her pulse was still unnaturally fast. She wasn't sure if it was the proximity of her escort that was causing this or being obliged to meet so many members of society. She still had the scars from her unpleasant debut many years ago.

Fletcher squeezed her hand in sympathy and then led her smoothly through the gawping crowd to the drawing room. The strangers were not the only ones to watch them closely. She saw Lord Wydale following their progress and his dark eyes narrowed in annoyance. His hard stare sent a shiver of apprehension down her spine.

Three hours later she had waltzed three times with her soon-to-be fiancé and felt like the belle of the ball. For the first time in her life she had danced with a man who could match her step for step and didn't make her feel clumsy. She had floated around the room in his arms, her face radiant. When she hadn't been dancing with Fletcher she had been at his side listening to him talking knowledgeably about politics and the latest *on dits* from Town.

'Come, sweetheart, allow me to take you in to supper. I believe that Mrs Fox and Edmund are already at a table.'

'I'm too excited to eat, but I would like a cooling drink of lemonade.'

The evening passed too quickly and like Cinderella she found herself in her coach just before midnight. Her mother tapped her archly on the arm with her folded fan.

'My dear, you have made a match of it. Anyone can see that Mr Reed is besotted with you.'

Eliza sighed. 'And I with him, Mama. I believe he will make me an offer after our party next week.'

'I should think so,' Edmund said from the corner of the darkened vehicle. 'If he didn't after his display of partiality this evening I should be obliged to call him out.'

This piece of nonsense sent Eliza into a fit of giggles and sent Edmund into a dudgeon. He spoke no more. Her mother slept leaving her to dream about her forthcoming wedding and trying to imagine what she might expect to experience in the marriage bed. The very thought sent her temperature soaring and she had recourse to use her fan vigorously in order to restore her composure.

★ ★ ★

'Tell me again about the party, Liza, please . . . please.'

'Sarah I've already told you four times — you must know what happened as well as I do.' Eliza set down her sewing with a smile. 'I know, why don't you tell me about it and then I can listen?'

She was able to allow her mind to wander during this recital, back to the magical moment when Fletcher had swept her around the ballroom making her feel like one of Sarah's princesses. A sharp pain in her thigh caused her to look down. Inadvertently she had attempted to stitch her leg to her embroidery.

She stared at the material. What had possessed her to attempt to embroider a cushion cover? She knew as much about sewing as she did about preserving fruit — which was absolutely nothing. Tossing the cloth to one side she jumped up startling her sister who was attempting to build a house out of bricks.

As her walls tumbled down, Sarah sighed with frustration. 'I was trying to build a castle. Do you think that Lord Wydale has a castle? Is he coming to see me again?'

Eliza frowned. She'd hoped that her sister had forgotten her infatuation with the repellent lord. The sooner Fletcher spoke to her mother and made their engagement official the better; then this debt of honour could be settled and forgotten.

★ ★ ★

The days until the party dragged. Fletcher had warned her he would not be able to visit before then as his host and hostess had a series of engagements planned from which he could not extract himself without appearing uncivil.

Friday eventually arrived and she was downstairs in her oldest clothes at first light helping to arrange the flowers in the ballroom and dining room. Her mother found her finishing a stunning arrangement of garden blooms for the enormous fireplace in the drawing room.

'Eliza, you must have been up with the lark. The flowers are wonderful, my dear, but it's time for you to go up and change then take yourself off for a gallop around the park. You need to release some of your energy, for you're coiled as tightly as a spring.'

'There, I've finished. I shall do as you suggest, Mama, and have my breakfast when I return. I'm so glad you decided to hold this party early. Waiting until eight o'clock for our guests to arrive would have been purgatory.'

★ ★ ★

At half past four the house was shining, the staff in their best, the stables ready to receive the carriages, and the Fox family resplendent in full evening dress. Eliza had chosen tonight to wear her favourite gown, a damask silk creation with a demitrain. As she juggled with her fan, reticule and the ribbon that held her train from under her feet, she was beginning to wish she had selected something less elaborate.

'Liza, you look like a pink princess tonight. I think Lord Wydale will like you better than me.' Sarah tugged at the lemon-yellow sash that encircled the high-waist of her delicate dimity gown. 'Mama, why can't I have a dress like that?'

'You have been warned, Sarah. If you cannot remain quiet then Jane is going to take

117

you upstairs and you will miss the dancing. I know that I have promised you may have one dance with Edmund, but that depends on your good behaviour.'

'I'm sorry, Mama, I shall be good now.'

Eliza released her breath with a sigh. She thought it was a bad idea to allow her sister to attend this event. Sarah's obsession with Wydale could make things decidedly awkward. She wouldn't put it past that loathsome man to single Sarah out just to embarrass the family.

'Edmund, can I have a private word, before our guests arrive?' Her brother followed her out into the hallway and across to the study.

'I can guess what it is, Liza.' He was grinning at her and she knew he was expecting to be told that Fletcher was to make her an offer that night.

'I doubt that you can. I am concerned about Sarah's interest in Lord Wydale. Can I ask you to keep an eye on that man? After all he would not be here — '

'You have no need to remind me, Liza. If that man goes within arm's reach of my little sister he will regret it.'

'There will be no need for heroics; I am only asking you to ensure that Sarah does not get out of her depth.' Impulsively she stepped across and embraced him. 'Anyway, if you

118

hadn't gambled away our house I should not have met Mr Reed, so I forgive you.'

The sound of wheels on gravel alerted them to the arrival of their first guests. Glancing down to check her hems were straight and her *décolletage* in place Eliza ran back to join her mother in the drawing room. The hall was too narrow to greet arrivals so Mrs Fox waited in the drawing room.

Several local families had arrived and some were gossiping happily at the far end of the long drawing room whilst others had drifted out onto the terrace to enjoy the early evening sunshine. The French doors in both the drawing room and ballroom had been left open for this very reason.

Sarah was sitting upright on a small gilt chair, her companion by her side, drinking in every moment of her first evening event. Eliza smiled at her sister just as Fletcher and Lord Wydale wandered in. She had no idea the impact she made on both men.

'My lord, Mr Reed, how kind of you to come. Do you wish me to introduce you to any of the guests?'

Lord Wydale merely nodded, a supercilious smile on his handsome face, but Fletcher bowed deeply. 'Good evening, madam. We are honoured to have been invited to your delightful home.' He grinned at Edmund and moved quickly to stand in front of Eliza.

She sank into a deep curtsey and he reached out, capturing her hand then raising it to his lips. As he kissed her knuckles she felt a flash of heat and unconsciously swayed towards him. His mouth quirked in response and he drew her to his side, effectively cutting Wydale out. Eliza saw the venomous look that was directed at her partner's back and for a second her happiness dimmed.

But there was no time to worry — she was soon caught up in a flurry of locals all eager to be introduced to the two wealthy gentlemen from Town. It was not often that members of the *ton* graced a local soirée. In the excitement of the evening, the delight of waltzing three times with Fletcher, Eliza forgot to keep an eye on her sister. When supper was announced she remembered and looked around anxiously, but Sarah was not present.

'Fletcher, I have to find Sarah. I asked Edmund to keep an eye on her, but as you can see he's dancing with a local beauty.'

'We shall search together, sweetheart.'

Sarah was nowhere inside and neither was Lord Wydale. With sinking heart Eliza hurried through the crowd and out on to the terrace. Although it was well lit with flambeaus, there were areas of shadow in which couples could be private. She prayed that Sarah was not amongst them.

'Fletcher, where is she? And where is Wydale?'

'Relax, my love, he's safely ensconced in a game of chance in the study. Several of the gentlemen went through to play an hour ago. Wherever your sister is, she's not with him.'

'Thank God! If they are not together then I am no longer worried. I expect Sarah's retired. Mama said she was to go up before supper.'

She turned to go back inside, but his hand restrained her. 'Please, don't go back just yet. We have had no time together tonight.'

'What flummery! We have spent the entire evening in each other's company.'

His words brushed over her cheeks like gossamer. 'I'm talking about private time, darling girl.'

Before she could protest she was in his arms and his firm lips closed over hers. This time she knew what to do and softened her mouth allowing him access to the moist interior. She leant against him, her limbs too weak to support her, wondering about the strange heat that pooled in her most intimate place.

It was he who drew the embrace to a halt. He untangled her arms and gently held her away. 'Enough, my darling, we have already overstepped what's even permissible between betrothed couples. And we're not even that at the moment.'

It was several minutes before Eliza felt ready to answer. She allowed the cool of the house wall to soothe her overheated body and the gentle breeze to fan her scarlet cheeks.

'Fletcher, I don't understand what happens to me when you hold me. I become a different person — am no longer in control of myself.'

'It's called passion, sweetheart. Something best enjoyed in the privacy of a bedroom — and between man and wife.'

They heard footsteps and breathy giggles approaching and stiffened, but whoever it was passed them by, more concerned with their own clandestine meeting than looking for others doing the same.

'Shall we go in for supper?' Eliza was pleased her voice sounded quite normal.

'Of course.' He tucked her hand into his arm and they strolled, in complete accord, back through the French doors and into a nearly deserted drawing room.

'Everyone must have repaired to the supper table.' Eliza pulled her hand free in order to smooth back her hair and shake out invisible creases from her gown.

'Eliza, I shall come tomorrow to speak to your mother.'

'So I should hope, sir,' she relied archly, 'after the liberties you have taken tonight.'

He laughed out loud. 'Baggage! Shall I ride with you first?'

'Yes, please join me. Shall we go out at seven-thirty — no one will be up then?'

The matter settled to both their satisfaction they rejoined the company and when she eventually fell into her bed Eliza was incandescent with joy. Tomorrow she would become the future wife of the most wonderful man in the world. She fell asleep certain that her future was settled and all her worries were over.

10

The next morning was overcast and heavy rain threatened. Eliza was not deterred and headed for the stables nonetheless. A little rain had never bothered her before and the thought that Fletcher would be joining her gave her the added impetus to brave the elements. However as she reached the archway the heavens opened and she was forced to return, at a run, to the house. Disappointed that Fletcher would not come in the rain she wandered disconsolately to the breakfast parlour. Maybe it was an April shower and they could go out for their ride later on.

Fletcher was halfway to Grove House when the downpour started and he too turned back. He could not present himself to Mrs Fox dripping wet. Back at the inn he hurried upstairs to speak to Wydale. He had decided to confront him about the debt and demand that he allowed the matter to be settled between them. He knocked on Wydale's sitting room and walked in not waiting for permission to do so.

'Ah, there you are, Fletcher, old fellow.

When the landlady told me you had gone out in this weather I could hardly credit the information. Where have you been in such a downpour?'

Fletcher closed the door behind him with slow deliberation. It was as if his eyes were finally open and he could see the man lounging before him as he truly was. There was not a spark of humanity in his face to temper the ruthlessness.

'I have been to Grove House to see Miss Fox. I intend to buy back what you took from that young man. I will not let you turn them out of their house. You will sell those vowels to me, it matters not to you where the thirty thousand guineas come from; either way you'll be rich.'

He saw the habitual sneer spread across the man's face. 'So that is how the land lies, is it? You have taken a shine to the older sister. Excellent. You may have her, but I intend to have the younger one.'

Fletcher felt a surge of white-hot rage pour through him. He clenched his fists, holding himself in check with difficulty. He managed to keep his voice even, hiding his feelings.

'Sarah is not available and especially not to someone like you.'

Wydale shrugged. 'Did you think I had not realized she's a simpleton? I do not intend to marry the chit, merely amuse myself. She will have no need for conversation when lying flat on her back.'

Fletcher stretched forward and seized him by the throat, lifting him by one hand from his chair, sending the breakfast crockery crashing to the floor. Without a second thought his right hand swung back to smash into the grinning face of his erstwhile friend.

The force of the blow hit Wydale's nose with a satisfying crunch and blood splattered his white shirt front. Fletcher wanted to finish the job, to smash his face to a pulp, but somehow restrained himself. How could he ever have considered this man worthy of his friendship? He was an animal, no, worse than that, for animals did not deliberately misuse each other.

Unable to speak, Wydale's eyes said it all. Never had Fletcher seen such hatred, such malevolence in a human being. He had made an implacable enemy and, despite his superior size, felt a shiver of apprehension slither down his spine.

He towered over the prostrate body. 'If you go near Miss Fox or her sister I shall kill you.'

On impulse he turned and snatched up Wydale's topcoat, which was hanging carelessly from the back of a chair. He reached inside and located the envelope that contained the IOUs. Without a second thought he pushed them into his own pocket and strode out.

He would never acknowledge Wydale again and none of his friends would either. When he was next in Town he would make sure he was blackballed from all the clubs. Wydale was the ruined man now, not Edmund Fox.

He returned to his rooms and told Sam to pack his bags. He wished to distance himself from the vile creature in the next chamber. 'I'm going over to Grove House. Have things ready for my return.'

His horse had been rubbed down and was resaddled in a jiffy by his groom, Billy.

'It's stopped raining, sir. Quite pleasant out now. You'll not get wet again this morning.'

'Thank you, Billy. I shall be back later and we shall be leaving here. I'll let you know where we're going when I return. But we're not going with Lord Wydale in his carriage. I'm afraid you'll have to make your own way back to Town.'

Fletcher cantered down the long drive to Grove House and discovered that Eliza had already left for a belated ride. He knew exactly where she would be waiting for him — in the folly on the other side of the lake. Sure enough she was sitting inside, her lovely face alight with happiness at his appearance.

After a blissful few minutes on the bench Fletcher sat back, caressing her hand. 'My love, I have left an envelope for Edmund at the house. It contains his IOUs. He is out of debt, you no longer need to sell your shares.'

'I don't understand. How did you persuade him to give them up?' She saw a flash of something dark and dangerous in his eyes, but he didn't answer her question.

'There are formalities to be endured.' He grinned. 'Is Edmund your guardian by any chance?'

'Whatever made you think that? He has not reached his majority. I suppose officially an uncle that I didn't know existed until the other day, is head of the family. However I think it will suffice if we tell my mother and grandmother and anyone in your family who needs to know.'

'I have no relatives I wish to inform, sweetheart. I cannot believe that you've agreed to marry me when you know so little about me.'

'Well, now's the time to rectify that omission. Do you really have no family? You have met all of mine, apart from Uncle Benjy, and I've not met him myself.'

'I have a father alive, he lives in solitary splendour at Longshaw, an enormous pile of masonry in Gloucestershire. I have not spoken to him for over fifteen years and have no intention of doing so now.'

Shocked to the core by his apparent callousness, she jumped up and moved away breaking the contact between them. 'How can you say that? Whatever bad feeling there is between you, presumably you are his only heir and any children we might have would be his grandchildren.'

He gave a snort of derision. 'And much he will care about that. When my mother and two older brothers died from the fever I no longer had any reason to return home. My parents married for love, a rare occurrence in the circles in which we move. However, after I was born there were complications and my parents were no longer able to share the marital bed. Another baby would have proved fatal. My mother poured her frustration into loving me and my two brothers, but my father turned his frustration into hating the baby that had caused this chasm.'

'How dreadful! To hate a baby which, through no fault of its own, had caused this separation. Surely, loving another human being does not rely entirely upon bedroom matters?'

'You're quite right, my dear. It does not, but for my father it was too much for him to bear; to be close to the wife he adored and not be able to share the love in a physical way. When I was seven I was sent away to a miserable school. It was there that I met Wydale, as I believe I told you before. He is two years my senior and he kept me alive during those unspeakable years.

My father would not allow me to come home so I was obliged to spend vacations at school, although occasionally other pupils offered me refuge at their homes during the summer. Wydale was another who was rejected by his family. It seems his father believes he is not his true son, his wife played him false with her lover and he was the result.'

'But he is the only son? Does that mean despite the difficulty of his conception he is his father's heir?'

'You have guessed the whole and that is where the canker lies. His father refuses to acknowledge him, and has done his best to ruin the estate and spend his inheritance. What is not entailed has been given away to charity and to distant relatives. When the earl finally turns up his toes Wydale will inherit nothing of any value apart from the title. It's hardly surprising he's a bitter man.'

'You have had a similar experience and it has not turned you into a black-hearted villain. You mentioned you have your own estate, shall we live there together?'

'Indeed we shall, my darling.' He smiled and raised his hand to smooth a stray lock of hair from her face. 'I'm afraid that I am impossibly rich. I inherited from my maternal grandmother, and several other fortunes from childless relatives. Whatever my father's designs, he is not in a position to bankrupt me. I am, I believe, considered to be one of the most eligible bachelors around.'

She laughed out loud. 'I must say, sir, for an eligible bachelor, you have made a very odd choice of bride.'

He encircled her neck, pulling her towards him and she went willingly into his arms. After several wonderful minutes, he released her, holding her face in his strong hands, to place a final kiss on her parted lips.

'I have told you before, you're a truly beautiful woman, both inside and out. You have a figure that is voluptuous and, if I could persuade you to grow your hair, you would look like a Greek goddess.'

'A very tall Greek goddess; most women of my acquaintance are dark and dainty and they look at me as a freak show. I believe that is why I was happy to abandon dresses for britches when I took over running the estate on my father's death.'

'Well, I hope you will use your expert knowledge to assist me when we're wed. I have little knowledge of estate management and you shall be my guide.' His lips travelled lightly up her face and his eyes burned with something she now recognized. 'And I shall be your guide in other matters if you will let me?'

★ ★ ★

They cantered back to Grove House full of expectation and wonder. They had decided a long engagement would be pointless, they knew their own minds even after so short a time. Eliza had pointed out that she was approaching her quarter-century and would like to be married before she reached that milestone.

'I am ten years your senior, my dear, and it is high time I set up my nursery. So we're agreed? We shall be married as soon as we can persuade your mama.' He smiled at her.

She loved the way his eyes crinkled up at the corners; he was not a classically handsome man, not like her brother, but to her he was everything she had ever wanted. A sudden interesting, and indelicate thought, occurred to her.

'You mentioned you're eager to set up your

nursery, Fletcher. Can you imagine what our children will be like? We shall be accused of creating a race of giants.'

His roar of laughter sent his spirited stallion skittering sideways and by the time he had restored calm they were in the stable yard and the conversation ceased. They were met by the coachman and the two grooms, their faces etched with concern.

'Whatever's wrong? Has there been bad news?'

'You'd best go in, miss, there's a panic in the house. Miss Sarah and Jane went out more than two hours ago and have not returned.'

Fletcher was beside her and lifted her from the saddle. 'I'm sure there's nothing to worry about, my love, they're probably visiting friends.'

Eliza knew this could not be the case. When Jane took Sarah into the village they always followed a strict routine. They walked to the church, no more than a mile's distance, to place flowers on Papa's grave and then to the baker's to buy a cake. That was all and they were always back in less than an hour and a half. If they had been gone for two hours something must be wrong.

She burst into the drawing room, to see Edmund kneeling at his mother's side,

133

stroking her hands, and trying to offer comfort.

He looked up at her sudden entrance, his face pale. He signalled to them to go back out in order to converse in private. Once they were safely in the library Edmund told them what he knew.

11

'I have already visited the churchyard and the flowers they took are on the grave so Sarah and Jane definitely went there. When I checked at the baker's, they hadn't called in and no one saw them after they entered the churchyard.'

'Have you asked everyone in the vicinity?' Fletcher demanded.

'Yes, and I left my man Denver to continue making enquiries. He has yet to return.' His face had a pinched look and he seemed to have aged ten years since breakfast. 'I am certain Wydale has taken them but I cannot imagine why he should wish to do so. I thought he had had a change of heart when he returned my vowels to me.'

'I'm afraid that you're under a misapprehension, Mr Fox. I took the papers without his permission after I had broken his nose for making improper suggestions about Miss Sarah.'

Eliza stared from one man to the other. Sarah would be safe if Edmund had not been stupid enough to gamble. Sarah would be safe if Fletcher had not seen fit to break his

135

friend's nose and then steal the vowels from his pocket.

That it was Lord Wydale who had abducted her sister, she had not the slightest doubt. He would have his revenge if he could not have the property. She felt her heart shrivel and the fledgling love she'd formed for the tall man watching her through narrowed eyes, died within her.

'This débâcle is your fault. If you had not assaulted him, Mr Reed, and then stolen property from his jacket pocket, none of this would have happened. I lay the blame entirely on your shoulders.' She looked at him dispassionately and saw his cheeks pale as he understood that all was at an end between them.

'You are quite right to castigate me; it is my responsibility that this situation has arisen. But be sure, I shall return Miss Sarah to you unharmed.'

Eliza remained impassive, not impressed by his protestations. Hadn't he promised that no harm should come to any of them, indeed, given his word as a gentleman on this matter?

'Mr Reed, I believe that your interference has caused enough damage already. This is a family matter; it has nothing whatsoever to do with you. You are a stranger to us, kindly leave the house and do not return. We shall arrange things as we see fit.'

She saw Edmund flinch at her harsh words, but was unconcerned. She knew that Sarah's abductor would contact her, not because he wanted his money, but because he wanted to hurt both Edmund and Mr Reed.

She saw the man she thought she had loved nod briefly to her. 'Your servant, madam. Please convey my sympathy to Mrs Fox.' He said no more, just straightened his shoulders and strode out taking her happiness with him.

Edmund hurried off behind him and she did not bother to call him back. She had no time for either of them; she had to contact Mr Firmin at once and make sure she had a banker's draft made out to Lord Wydale waiting for when the summons came.

She rejoined her mother and grandmother in the drawing room, knowing what she had to tell them was the very last thing they wanted to hear. She braced herself for an outburst of anguish and sobbing. She told them both as gently as she could why Sarah had been taken.

'Are you saying, Eliza, that all this is Mr Reed's fault? If he had not interfered in the matter, Sarah would be safe at home with us now?'

'That's exactly what I'm telling you, Mama. The blame lies entirely with Edmund and Mr Reed. Between them they have caused this disaster. However, I have the money from the holdings coming any day, and I'm sure that Lord Wydale will accept that in exchange for Sarah's safety.'

'But she will be so frightened, she has never stayed away from home before and what if . . . and what if . . . ?'

Mrs Fox could not finish, but Eliza knew exactly what she was referring to. 'Sarah will be frightened, there is nothing we can do about that. However, remember, Mama, she has Jane with her. His lordship would not have taken Jane as well if he had intended anything improper to happen. He's using her as a bargaining tool; he wants his money and knows he will never get it now Edmund has burned the IOUs.'

Mrs Dean patted her daughter's hand. 'Hannah, my dear, you must be strong. Eliza is right; that wretched man will deal with Eliza, not Edmund nor Mr Reed. All we have to do is wait for his message to come.'

'I shall call Reverend Clarkson to pray with us, we need all the help from the Almighty that we can get.'

Eliza shook her head. 'No, Mama. We must keep this matter to ourselves. Only the staff know and they are loyal and will not breathe a word outside Grove House. We know that

Sarah will be unharmed, but do you think anyone else will believe that?'

The older women exchanged worried glances and then looked back at Eliza. Her mother spoke, her voice thick with tears. 'Then we must pray together, my dear. Pray that somehow good can come out of this evil.'

★　★　★

Eliza visited the office of her lawyers in Colchester, stoically enduring the uncomfortable carriage drive of several miles. She returned with the knowledge that the required document would be with her when the lawyer returned from London. She prayed it would be sooner rather than later.

She had not told anyone that she believed it was not only the money that Wydale would demand. He wanted revenge on both the men who had shown him such contempt. Taking Sarah was just the first step; what he intended was to compromise her. By doing this he would destroy the happiness of Mr Reed, and her brother.

Mr Reed would never take a woman as his wife who had been besmirched by another man. Eliza understood quite clearly that she would be damaged goods when she returned, but that was a small price to pay if it safely reunited her family.

She would never feel the same way about Edmund again. She had indulged his every whim, as had both her mother and grandmother. From now on he would have to manage on his own. He would not be welcome at Grove House until he had become a man who could be trusted. The fact that he was the owner of her home, and had more right to be there than she did, did not bother her.

Edmund had vanished. He had returned to his chambers and collected his belongings and left, presumably with Mr Reed, to search for Sarah.

★   ★   ★

The day after Sarah's disappearance Mr Firmin arrived with the bank draft that Eliza was waiting for.

'Is Mr Fox not here? You must be so relieved that he can pay his debts so easily.'

'No, sir, he has gone away with his friend Mr Reed for a few days. I thank you for your concern, but the matter has been settled and we shall have no further need of your services. I appreciate your promptness in this matter.'

Eliza read the document carefully, making sure that there could be no flaw found in it

140

when she handed it over. Satisfied it had been drawn up exactly as she wished, she hurried upstairs to make her preparations.

She needed to remain strong, pretend that she was just awaiting the summons from Lord Wydale and would be able to go at once to collect Sarah. Later that day a closed carriage arrived outside Grove House. Eliza had been expecting it. She already had her bag packed, and one for Sarah as well.

She had asked Ann, who had been acting as her personal maid in Jane's absence, to prepare the bags for Jane and herself. Eliza was waiting in the drawing room, bag at her side, when Mrs Green appeared in the doorway.

'There is a note for you, Miss Fox, the driver says as he'll wait.'

Eliza recognized the handwriting, it was that of Sarah's companion, Jane. She ripped it open and quickly scanned the contents.

Dear Miss Fox
Miss Sarah and I are being well looked after and have come to no harm. Lord Wydale requests that you return with the carriage. He says that you have something of his that he wishes you to return. We are alone in the house at present.
Signed
Jane Smith, Miss.

Eliza's summons had come. She was glad she was alone, her relatives had taken the carriage into the village to call into the church, believing that their prayers would be more effective if spoken in God's house.

She looked up to see the housekeeper hovering near the door. 'This is the message I was expecting from Jane, Mrs Green. As you can see I am ready to leave. Please tell Mrs Fox that I shall be away overnight but expect to return with Miss Sarah safe and sound tomorrow.'

Ann appeared at the housekeeper's side, having also heard the carriage arrive. The girl picked up her bag and tucked it under her arm. Eliza hurried out to the coach noticing that the blinds were drawn. The coachman sitting on the box had his collar turned up and his hat pulled down over his ears making it impossible to see his face.

The second man opened the door and politely handed Eliza up the steps. Her maid followed and placed the bags on the floor between them. Eliza glanced down and even in the near darkness of the closed carriage she could see that the handles on the inside of the doors had been removed. It would be impossible to escape even if they had wished to. She was a captive, and only yards from her own home.

Sinking back on the squabs, she pulled her warm cloak around her shoulders, glad that the deep brimmed bonnet she had chosen hid her expression from the anxious girl beside her. She felt the coach rock as the second man climbed up on the box next to the driver and then she heard the whip crack and the four horses leaned into the traces and the coach moved away. Eliza closed her eyes, grateful that the blinds were down and no one could see her disgrace.

She didn't see the two men, mounted on sturdy horses, trot out of the drive and follow behind the carriage. Eliza believed she was totally alone, that the safety of her sister rested entirely on her shoulders.

The journey seemed interminable, the coach although well sprung, rocked and bumped over potholes and ruts which told her one thing, they were not travelling on the toll-road, but by side lanes. She had far too much time to dwell on what might have been. How could she have imagined herself to have fallen in love with Mr Reed? It was hardly surprising that their love had taken wing at this disaster when it had flown in so unexpectedly. She supposed that she must resign herself to a miserable life as a doting aunt to Edmund's future progeny.

By the time the carriage finally rocked to a

standstill she was bruised and sore from the three hours she had spent inside. Eliza smiled across at her maid, hoping to reassure her.

'Ann, you must do whatever you are told. Do not argue, for your very life might depend on it, and the lives of others.'

As soon as she had spoken, she realized her words had terrified the girl. She watched her face pale, and thought she would have to deal with a fainting companion as well as everything else.

'Come now, Ann. You knew when you came we were not going on a shopping expedition to Colchester or a jaunt around the countryside. You knew that we were responding to the bidding of a dreadful man in order to rescue Miss Sarah.'

'Yes, miss, I beg your pardon. Of course I did know, it's just hearing it put so baldly gave me quite a turn. I'm steady now.'

Eliza slipped her hand into her cloak pocket and her fingers closed around the polished butt of a small pistol that was primed and ready to fire. She might be naïve, but she was not stupid. She had come prepared for every eventuality. She also had sewn a tiny stiletto knife into her chemise. This delicate blade in its finely tooled leather scabbard had been brought back from India by her father. He had intended her to use it

144

as a letter opener, but she believed it might prove to be invaluable.

She had never harmed another human being, but hoped that if it meant a choice between her life, or that of Lord Wydale, she would not hesitate. She was determined not to let him sense how terrified she was. She had to remain strong, set an example for Sarah who had already endured more than a day's captivity. Ann, although a sensible country girl, was not used to mixing with villains and abductors.

She heard someone pushing the handle back into the empty hole in the door and then it swung open. The man who had incarcerated them several hours before leant in and flicked down the carriage steps. Without a word, he stepped back, and assisted her descent. She turned to collect her bag but Ann spoke quietly behind her.

'You go on, miss, I can manage the bags. Go and see Miss Sarah, I'll be along directly.'

12

Eliza looked around expecting to see a dismal, derelict farmhouse, or maybe a ruined castle, but not this. The carriage was standing in a neatly trimmed turning circle, the gravel swept, weed free, the greensward closely manicured. She glanced up at the house itself. It was a mixture of Elizabethan and more recent construction. This also was in excellent repair, leaded windows sparkling in the evening sun.

Nothing could be further than the image she had carried in her head for the past few hours. This was a home, not a hideout for people who had been abducted by an evil man. Had she been mistaken? Had Sarah gone with his lordship willingly and was a guest and not a captive?

The uncomfortable pressure in her bladder reminded her that it was several hours since she had used the commode. It was going to be hard to maintain her dignity until she had been given access to a private place to relieve herself. She almost smiled at her thoughts; they were hardly the wild imaginings of someone arriving to sacrifice herself in order to save her sister.

She heard Ann shuffling up behind her; no one had come out to help them with their bags, which was odd, considering that the house must have several staff in order to keep it in its immaculate condition.

'This looks all right, miss. Not what I expected, I can tell you. I reckon Miss Sarah and Jane have been having a bit of a holiday here and maybe we've been worrying without grounds.'

Eliza drew breath to answer when the front door opened and a stony-faced woman dressed in crisp black, appeared followed by a footman suitably bewigged and a parlour maid in his wake.

'Good afternoon, Miss Fox, if you should like to come this way I shall show you to your rooms. I'm sure you will wish to refresh yourself before coming downstairs and being reunited with Miss Sarah and her companion.'

Speechless Eliza nodded, and watched as the two members of staff hurried down the steps and removed the bags from Ann's hands.

'If you would care to follow me, madam, his lordship suggests that you have an apartment adjacent to your sister.'

Eliza fell in behind the tall, thin woman who oozed disapproval from every pore of her sallow skin. Exactly what had Lord Wydale told his staff? This was obviously a respectable establishment, not somewhere a madman would incarcerate his victims. Bemused at this turn-around in circumstances, she hurried along behind the housekeeper, who had neglected to introduce herself, into the interior of the building.

There was a spacious entrance hall, a large square with a floor of black-and-white marble tiles, far grander than the one at Grove House. Stairs curved up elegantly on one side and it was to these that she was led.

Everywhere she looked there were signs of good housekeeping. Carpets were freshly scrubbed, not worn in the slightest and the banisters were polished to such a high degree she saw her hand's reflection as she clutched the banister on the way up. Her chambers were in the guest wing on the first floor — presumably the reception rooms were on the ground floor as at home.

She was whisked along passageways, past several closed doors. The light from the large rectangular window, this one modern and not with the small leaded panes of the front of the house, threw ample light, allowing her to look with interest at three family portraits as she passed.

There was something about them that she found unsettling. Yes! She stopped, and stared at the third of the men in a white ruff with a little beard. She knew exactly what it was: these men were all blonde and blue-eyed, Wydale was dark. These were not his ancestors, this was not his family home.

Was this another property he had snatched from some unwitting young man? She shuddered at the thought. For some reason she did not even consider that the property was his, or that he could have a friend prepared to lend him this place. She remembered what Fletcher had told her, that Wydale was impecunious, had been made so by his dreadful father, and needed Grove House and its estates in order to refill his pockets.

The housekeeper stopped abruptly and opened a door. She stepped to one side so that Eliza could enter. A charming parlour was revealed. There were comfortable seats and a cheery fire crackled in the grate. Her feet sank into the thick carpet as she walked.

'Your bedchamber and dressing room are through there, Miss Fox. Miss Sarah and her companion are waiting for you in the garden room downstairs. I shall leave a footman outside the door to conduct you when you are ready to go down.' The woman dipped her head, and stalked out of the room.

Eliza wasted no time, but fled into the

bedchamber and thence into the dressing-room. Ten minutes later she was recovered and her face washed, bonnet and gloves removed, cloak hanging in the commodious closet, and ready to go.

Leaving Ann to unpack the few belongings she had brought with her she went through her sitting room and out into the passageway. As promised, a young footman was waiting. She got the distinct impression he was leering, and felt herself colour under his scrutiny. He was a servant; he had no right to look at a guest in that way.

As she followed him back downstairs she was forced to the conclusion that perhaps her sudden appearance had been explained to the staff as being the arrival of the owner's mistress. But how had he explained Sarah and Jane's presence here? Surely staff did not believe he was running two such relation-ships, and both from the same family?

Whatever it was, it was as bad as she had feared in some ways and far better in others. Her lips twitched involuntarily; she supposed it was better to be ruined in comfortable surroundings than otherwise.

The footman flung open the door and stepped to one side. He didn't bother to announce her. Eliza found herself in a room full of sunlight and the sweet smell of orange blossom. It was obviously the garden room: three sides were glazed and exotic plants and flowers grew in abundance everywhere. Doors opened onto a wide terrace and it was there that she spotted her sister and her maid.

Sarah had obviously been watching and she heard her cry out in pleasure. This wasn't a girl terrified out of her wits, but someone enjoying a visit away from home but pleased to see her nevertheless.

'Liza, you've come at last. Lord Wydale promised me that I could have anything I wanted, and I said that I wanted you.'

Eliza glanced past her sister trying to see Jane's expression. 'Darling, Sarah, I'm so glad to see you, and looking so well. Where did you get that lovely gown? You came away with nothing, and here you are dressed in the first-stare of fashion.'

Delighted at the compliment, her sister spun round like the child she was, exposing her silk-covered ankles and matching slippers to anyone in the vicinity. 'Dear Lord Wydale got me a closetful of them. I have lots and lots of gowns to choose from as well as all the other things I need to look pretty.'

'Come and sit down, Sarah, and tell me how you come to be here. We have been so worried about you. Mama and Grandmamma have been beside themselves. Why did you

151

disappear like that?'

'Jane and I met Lord Wydale in the church, didn't we, Jane, and he said if I liked to I could come and stay with him.'

'But you hardly know him, Sarah. What ever possessed you to rush off and stay with a strange gentleman? You have never even been away from home on your own before.'

Sarah frowned and pouted. 'Dear Lord Wydale said you would be cross with me. But I don't care. I'm a grown-up lady now, he told me, and it's not right you keep me shut up in the house like a baby. He says I should wear pretty dresses and dance and attend parties.'

'I see. It would appear that Lord Wydale has had a great deal to say on the matter. Never mind, sweetheart, I'm glad that you've enjoyed yourself, but I'm here to take you home. Mama is most anxious to see you.'

Instantly Sarah was on her feet. 'I'm not going home, not with you. I'm staying here with dear Lord Wydale. I am to be his princess. He says I can stay here forever and do exactly as I please.'

Eliza stood up, realizing that her opponent was far cleverer than she had given him credit for. He had enticed her sister away with promises of things that she had been denied. Sarah was physically an adult, and would respond to his masculinity even though she didn't understand why. She could hardly drag Sarah home if she was unwilling.

Making an effort to steady her voice, not show her disquiet, she asked the all-important question. 'Sarah, where is his lordship now? I had expected him to be here to greet me.'

'He has gone to Town to fetch his friends back because there's going to be a party here, and you and I are to be the most important guests. Do you know he has bought me a beautiful evening gown, just like the one I saw in a fashion plate?'

Eliza felt sick to her stomach. Finally she understood what game he was playing. Whatever this house was, it was not used to seeing such goings-on, that was obvious from the attitude of the staff. She had to speak to Jane privately, discover exactly what was happening.

'Ann is upstairs; she has bought a bag of your things, Sarah. I don't suppose such a grown-up girl as you wants to see her dolls, but if you do, they are in the chambers that I have been allocated.'

Sarah was sunny again. 'I do want to see them, I do. Jane, take me upstairs please. I want to play with my dollies right now.'

Jane spoke for the first time. 'Of course I will, miss. Then you can show Ann where we are sleeping, and the big closet where you have hung all your new gowns. Then I'll come down and tell Miss Eliza what has been happening.'

Sarah seemed quite happy with this idea and Eliza watched the two of them vanish through the door. She was left alone in a place in which one should feel happy, but she felt wretched. She could see no way out of this. Wydale obviously wasn't interested in the money — if he had such a grand property he had been lying about his finances.

She had come with a bank draft in her reticule, determined to make the ultimate sacrifice only to find Sarah perfectly happy and everything on the surface appearing as normal. Wydale had out-manoeuvred her. He had no need to harm either of them physically; all he had to do was invite his friends — his male friends — down to wherever this was and both Sarah and she would be tarnished forever.

Edmund would be ruined also; he could never go to Town again; would not even be able to buy a commission in the army to get away from the disgrace. Although they wouldn't lose Grove House word of this would soon be all over Dedham, Wydale would make sure of that. They would no longer be received anywhere. She sank into the nearest armchair unable to think straight.

Somehow she had found it easier to prepare herself for violence, for ravishment, but this insidious use of comfort and good manners was far worse than being forcibly ruined. Both of them remaining innocent, but unable to prove it, would be the best revenge he could have.

Before too long Jane returned as eager to talk about what had transpired over the last two days as Eliza was to hear her news.

'I'm that sorry, Miss Fox, this is all my fault. I knew how Miss Sarah imagined herself to be in love with his lordship. I should never have allowed her to go over and speak to him when we met him in the churchyard.'

'So Sarah approached him, not the other way round?'

'Yes, miss, I'm afraid it was like that. Miss Sarah ran over, you know the way she does, and all but threw herself into his arms she was so pleased to see him. He was a perfect gentleman, I'm forced to admit. He bowed and didn't in any way behave as he shouldn't.'

'But how did you end up in his carriage being taken away without clothes or permission?'

Jane wrung her hands. 'You see, it was like

this. I couldn't hear what they were saying, but Miss Sarah was nodding and smiling and Lord Wydale turned and she placed her arm on his, just the way you do with a gentleman. I was forced to run after them in order to keep up.' The girl stopped, unable to carry on. Eliza waited for her to recover.

'His carriage was just out of sight, in the lane beside the churchyard. Before I knew what was happening Miss Sarah had jumped in. She called out to me that we were going for a ride that I could come with her or stay behind, it was up to me. Obviously I'd no choice, Miss Fox. I couldn't let her go by herself and that evil man knew I couldn't.' Eliza pushed herself upright and crossed the room to embrace the agitated girl. This débâcle wasn't Jane's fault.

She decided it would be better to hear the rest of the story unfold while she was sitting down. She had walked the aches out of her cramped legs by pacing up and down the room during the ten minutes or so she had waited for Jane to join her.

'Let's sit down, Jane. Out of the sun, where we can be private.' For some reason she felt as if the very plants were eavesdropping.

'Well, miss, we travelled alone in the carriage. That man must have ridden behind. At first I wasn't too bothered, thought he had just offered to give Miss Sarah a drive, you know how she likes to go out in a carriage. But, as time passed, and the landscape became unfamiliar, I realized we were in a real pickle.'

'Did you halt anywhere that you were recognized? Were the blinds up or down on the windows?'

'The blinds were up and Miss Sarah waved and laughed at everyone. I'm afraid that she was seen in the carriage by more than one person who recognized her. Eventually we pulled into a coaching inn and were taken into a private room. We were given an excellent luncheon, but saw no sign of Lord Wydale. I thought of trying to run away, but I had no money with me and had no idea where we were, I thought it best to continue.

Miss Sarah seemed quite unbothered by the whole thing and thought it a great adventure. She told me that he had promised she could come and stay with him and be his princess and wear lovely dresses and go to parties just like a grown-up.'

Eliza had heard enough. Everything Jane had told her confirmed what she had deduced for herself. It had been his intention all along for Sarah's visit to be public knowledge. So why had he brought her here in secrecy? It didn't make sense.

'Has Lord Wydale been here with you all this time?'

The girl shook her head. 'No, Miss Fox. We haven't seen him since we arrived. The housekeeper, not a friendly soul, has looked after us well. It's she who told Miss Sarah that he's returning tomorrow with friends from London.'

'In which case, we have twenty-four hours to think of a way out of this. Once he arrives with his friends it will be too late, the damage will be done.' Eliza raised her hand to prevent Jane's interruption. 'I know, Jane, Miss Sarah's reputation is ruined, but as everyone in Dedham knows she's of limited ability, they will not hold it against her. She will never contract a marriage, so whether she has lost her reputation or not, is immaterial. It is me that he wishes to disgrace in public. I had a season in London, Edmund is already a member of Brooks's and several other gentlemen's clubs. I shall be recognized at once.'

Eliza jumped to her feet and began her restless walking again; it had seemed so simple this morning. She had the money to give him and was prepared to do anything to save her sister — now everything had altered.

Wydale obviously wasn't interested in the money, he just wanted to make sure that her

158

family name was dragged through the mire and that Mr Reed's happiness was ruined.

She had been resigned to her fate when she thought she had no option, but now she could see a glimmer of hope. Perhaps she could come up with a way to remove herself and Sarah from wherever they were before they were seen.

Her first task was to discover the name of the establishment and its exact whereabouts. There would be no point asking the housekeeper; maybe one of the outside staff might be more amenable. Unlike Jane she had come prepared and had a purse full of coins — more than enough to bribe a stable boy and buy them all seats on a mail coach.

She smiled at Jane. 'Have you managed to discover where we are?'

'No, miss, but something one of the chambermaids let slip makes me think it's not many miles from London. Lord Wydale is expected to drive down in an afternoon, so it can't be that far.'

'Excellent. If we are close to Town then there must be a coaching inn within walking distance. I have the funds to pay for our passage — all we have to do is discover in which direction to go.'

Jane shook her head. 'That's not the problem, miss. It's Miss Sarah — you'll not persuade her to come away. She's being treated like royalty — everything she wants they fetch for her — all smiles and curtsies. She's under that man's spell and will never return willingly to Grove House, not unless something scares her badly enough to want her mama.'

13

Fletcher was not going to accept that everything was over between them. Eliza would not forgive or allow him to make amends at the moment. There was nothing he could do whilst Sarah was in Wydale's clutches; however, once things were on an even keel he would come back and try and persuade her to rethink her ultimatum. He was not a man who gave in easily. He had found the woman he wanted to spend the rest of his life with and was determined to marry her come what may.

He had reached the archway that led into the stable yard when he decided to wait for young Fox to catch him up.

'Mr Reed, sir, may I come with you? I am as unwelcome here at the moment as you are. The only way Eliza will ever forgive me my part in this is if I bring Sarah safely home.'

'Then we are on a joint mission, lad. I take it that you made enquiries in the village before returning to your mother and telling her that Sarah had been abducted?'

'Yes, I did. She was seen getting into a closed carriage with Jane and then several people saw her waving happily from the window obviously enjoying the excursion. There was no sign of Wydale; as far as anyone else knows she was merely engaging in a harmless pursuit.'

Fletcher frowned. And where the devil was Wydale in all this? If his intention had been to ruin Sarah's name then he should have been in the carriage with her. 'I have to go to Town. Can I leave you to arrange things here? If Eliza receives a message and leaves have two of your men follow.'

Edmund nodded vigorously. 'That I can do, sir. All the staff love Sarah and would do anything to bring her back safely. Why do you have to go to Town, if I am permitted to enquire?'

'I have to speak to friends. It is imperative to discover whether Wydale has been lying to me about his financial circumstances. He told me he had ruined you because he had the bailiffs at his heels, that all his estates were sold to pay his debts. If that is the case, then where does he intend to take Sarah? He had no time to arrange anything in advance.'

'You believe he still has a suitable property in which to hide her away?'

'I do. It's the only explanation. However, I have no idea of the whereabouts of such a place, but I have friends in London who can make enquiries for me.'

His black stallion had been rubbed down and walked around the yard to cool and was now waiting for him to mount. 'If the message comes before I return, make sure your men stay out of sight. And you must send word to me — or even better, come in person. You have my direction in Grosvenor Square?'

Edmund nodded. 'Yes, sir, I do. I wish you Godspeed and good luck with your mission.'

Fletcher looked down at the young man waiting anxiously in the yard. 'If you are *persona non grata* here, why don't you take my rooms at the Sun? I shall pay your shot.'

★　★　★

Fletcher decided to travel post. He returned to the Sun Inn where he brought his servants up-to-date with what was happening. He also wanted to know if downstairs gossip had perhaps let slip a clue about Wydale's intentions.

His valet Sam already had his bags packed. 'This is a rum do, sir. Word is all around the place that Sarah Fox has gone gallivanting in a carriage. His lordship's carriage is also missing — it don't take too much to work out the connection.'

163

'I had already guessed as much, Sam. I want you and Billy to return to Hendon Manor, Billy can ride my horse. I'm afraid you must hire a conveyance of some sort. It's a dratted nuisance that I chose to come in Wydale's carriage; I wish I had brought my own.'

'Never mind, sir. I reckon that I'll be back at the Manor by the time you return. Is there any particular message I'm to take to Mrs Percy?'

Fletcher thought for a moment. He knew he could rely on his manservant's absolute discretion, he had been with him for years; he was an ex-prizefighter he had sparred with when he first went about town. Previously there had been a supercilious man to attend to his wants, but he had discovered that he was in the employ of his father, was in fact a spy.

He had dismissed all his staff and then employed his own choices. Sam was an unlikely selection for a wealthy man-about-town, but he had soon learnt his trade and was as efficient at keeping his clothes pressed and his quarters clean as he was at escorting his current ladybird to and from her resting place.

'I believe that Wydale has taken Sarah as a ruse. I don't think he intends to harm her

164

whatever he might have said to the contrary. He's using her to entice Miss Fox to his side. It's she he intends to ruin and by so doing he believes he will have his revenge on me.'

'I guessed as much, sir. Like April and May you've been, since you met that young lady. I knew when it finally came, if you don't mind me saying, that you would choose your wife as quickly as you chose me. And you've never regretted that, have you, sir?'

Fletcher smiled reluctantly. 'Most of the time I haven't, Sam.' His man understood the message. He said no more, dropping to his knees to clean his master's riding boots and brush away every speck of mud and dust from his person.

'That will do.' Fletcher removed several gold coins from an inside pocket and handed them to Sam. 'This should be enough for your needs.' He realized he had still not explained why he wished him to go to his home and not join him in London. 'I believe that Miss Fox might need somewhere private to go and Hendon Manor will be ideal; the staff are loyal and I never receive visitors. She will be safe from prying eyes there until . . .'

He left the rest of his sentence unfinished. It was no business of Sam's that he intended to apply for a special licence whilst he was in London. If he did not manage to find out where Sarah was being held before Eliza went to join her, his beloved would lose her good name and be unable to return to Dedham until they were safely married and her reputation restored.

He knew she was as stubborn as he and might very well take some persuading, but she would, whether she wanted to or not. He would make quite sure she understood she had no choice. If her family were not to be ostracized as well then she would have to do as he suggested.

It did not occur to him that his demands might be seen by Eliza to be unpleasant. Although he was in love with her he did not fully understand how she felt about matters of honour. He truly believed that she would be glad to marry him. If she lost her good name in order to save Sarah, then he could not see any possible objection to his suggestion that she marry him.

He had been about town long enough to know that no woman would willingly sacrifice her reputation. He knew of at least one young lady of previously impeccable character who had been unwise enough to take a lover and, when the consequences became evident, had agreed to marry the most unsuitable of partners.

His face stiffened and his eyes blazed with

anger as he realized where his thoughts had been leading him. Up until that moment he had been glossing over the facts, thinking glibly about a licence, a need for privacy, but now he had let the awful truth in, he could not force it out again. Wydale would ravish Eliza without compunction, but would he then force her into marrying *him*?

Eliza was a woman like any other, so would she be only too happy to marry the man who had ruined her? Any child she might have would then be legitimate.

'Remember, tell my housekeeper to have everything prepared for Miss Fox. Sarah and her companion might well be with her, but I expect that they might prefer to return to Grove House. Also Mr Fox is taking these rooms, make sure they are paid for until the end of the month.'

Throwing his top coat over his arm he barged out of the bedchamber and took the stairs down to the flagstone entrance hall in threes. Outside in the yard he found Billy.

'Find me a hack, Billy, that can convey me to the nearest posting house.'

★ ★ ★

He had ample time to consider his next move during the tedious journey from

167

Colchester to London. Although he travelled by post-chaise this still involved stopping for refreshments and waiting whilst ostlers changed the horses.

Eventually he arrived at his destination and hailed a hackney to transport him to his townhouse in Grosvenor Square. The streets were teaming with people but he ignored them. He had decided exactly what he should do. Firstly he would change his garments then send someone reliable round to apply for the special licence at the Archbishop of Canterbury's office at Doctors' Commons. When he was refreshed he would visit each of his clubs. It was just possible that some of Wydale's acquaintances would be there.

It was early evening and most of the club members would be dining at home. The clubs and gaming hells did not fill up until much later, sometimes in the small hours when gentlemen had done the pretty with their wives at a ball and were then free to please themselves.

Wydale, of course, would have no such friends. His circle had become filled with hangers-on and the more unpleasant members of the *ton*. Fletcher knew that he should have severed the connection long since, but somehow the debt he owed from his

168

childhood had never seemed to be repaid. Fletcher had spent far less time with him than in former years, but on this occasion Wydale had sought him out and he had not had the heart to refuse.

The carriage rattled to a halt outside his palatial home. He jumped down and tossed a coin to the waiting driver, the man touched his hat with his whip and drove off, leaving Fletcher to run up the steps and hammer on his own front door.

Endean opened the door himself. For the first time in the ten years he had employed him his butler was completely at a loss.

'I have returned unexpectedly. Sam is going to Hendon Manor so I shall require Peterson to stand in for him. Also have my carriage brought round, I have several calls to make this evening.'

Endean finally recovered the power of speech. 'Yes, sir, at once. Shall you be staying long?'

'I doubt it. I expect to be leaving tomorrow or the next day.'

He was so used to the opulence of his surroundings he no longer noticed the spacious entrance hall or the wide galleried staircase, or the many footmen who were scurrying into position at his unexpected appearance. As one of the young men flattened himself to allow his master to pass by, something in his hand attracted Fletcher's attention. Good God! The man was holding a feather duster — he had thought that maids did all the cleaning, but obviously he was wrong. The young man's embarrassment only added to his amusement; he was surprised that he was able to smile when things were so bleak.

★ ★ ★

That evening he visited two less salubrious drinking places and was on his way to a third when he spotted someone he needed to talk to. He rapped sharply with his cane on the roof of the carriage and, as soon as it drew to a halt, he flung open the door and shouted across the street.

'Here, Jamieson, I need to speak to you urgently.'

The slightly overweight gentleman in his thirties jumped as if he'd been stuck with a large pin. For a moment Fletcher thought he was going to make a bolt for it, but he was beside the man and had grasped his elbow before he could make good his escape.

'Come along, Jamieson, I shall give you a ride to wherever you are going. We can converse in my carriage.' Giving the man no opportunity to refuse he bundled him across the street and into the vehicle. By this time the groom, who had been travelling at the rear of the carriage, was waiting to slam the door shut behind them.

In the gloom the other man's face showed that he was visibly shaken by this unexpected encounter. 'Well, Jamieson, I would like to know the answers to a few questions. I hope you're in a position to assist me?'

Fletcher had placed himself opposite, he leant forward, pushing his face close enough for the man to recoil in fear at what he saw there.

'What do you want to know, Reed? I shall answer if I can.'

'Excellent. Firstly you can tell me if you have seen Wydale.'

The man nodded vigorously. 'Yes, he was in Town earlier this evening, but he said he was too busy to stay and talk. I believe he was on his way to meet some acquaintances at a cockfight somewhere.'

Fletcher felt a wave of relief. If Wydale was already in Town, he could not have accompanied Sarah wherever he had sent her. She was safe as long as the man remained in sight. 'Good, an excellent answer. Now, the second question — do you know if Wydale still owns any properties?'

171

Jamieson now shook his head equally hard. 'He has told me that he recently acquired a neat little place somewhere in the country, a distant relative left it to him. However he didn't tell me where it was. Perhaps if you spoke to Sir Giles Mayhew, who knows him better than I, he might be able to give you the information you seek?'

Fletcher folded his arms and stared morosely at the man cowering back on to the squabs. Was he telling the truth? Would it be worth further investigation? 'Very well, thank you for your assistance. Where was it you were going? Allow me to convey you there.'

Jamieson shook his head. 'No, thank you. I much prefer to walk, it's good for my constitution.' Without giving Fletcher a chance to dispute the matter the coach door was open and the man almost fell out in his desire to escape further interrogation.

Fletcher rapped on the roof a second time indicating that he wished to continue his journey to Brooks's. He had two pieces of useful information, but what he really needed was the exact location of this *neat little property* that Wydale had neglected to mention he owned.

He scowled in the darkness as he realized Wydale had deliberately misled him. He had fleeced Fox because he wanted to, not because he had bailiffs hounding him. It was not only bailiffs that the bastard had to worry about now. By God, Wydale had better be ready to fight for his life when he finally caught up with him.

★ ★ ★

Eliza decided that the less time she spent downstairs being sneered at by the staff the better. Sarah said that she would be happy to join her in the pretty sitting room that adjoined her bedchamber. As it was still too early for supper Eliza suggested that they go for a walk around the garden.

The late afternoon sunshine was warm enough to make such an excursion pleasant. Sarah led the way, amazing Eliza at how well she knew her surroundings after such a short residence. They strolled around the formal gardens with Sarah chatting happily.

'Liza, have you looked in your closet and seen the lovely dresses you have been given to wear for the party?'

Eliza thought the less said about them the better. 'Yes, Sarah, they're very bright and cheerful. Are your evening gowns like mine?'

'No, Liza. His lordship said I was a lovely innocent princess and should wear pale colours, not reds and oranges like you.'

Eliza was determined that nothing would persuade her to don the hideous evening gowns that hung in her closet. They were obviously intended for a certain kind of lady. Wydale's intention was to make her look like Haymarket ware. She would rather wear a simple muslin afternoon dress for a ball than appear decked out in such a gown.

Sarah chatted on oblivious to her sister's disquiet. She was full of praise for the way the staff looked after her, the dresses she had been given, and the pony and trap that had been put at her disposal.

'A pony and trap? You are allowed to drive out in it alone, Sarah?'

'Oh yes, Liza. I've already been out in it three times. The pony's called Bubbles and he is very sweet and kind. He looks like my rocking horse in the nursery at home.' For the first time Eliza saw her sister's expression change to one of worry. 'Is my rocking horse still there? I hope everyone knows I am coming home very soon to tell them all about my lovely stay.'

Eliza felt a rush of relief. 'Of course your rocking horse is safe in your nursery, Sarah darling. And everybody knows you are having a delightful time, but they are all missing you dreadfully. Mama has sent me to bring you home so that they can hear all about your adventure.'

Sarah's smile vanished. Eliza realized she had made a grave error of judgement. 'I shan't come home until I've been to all the parties that Lord Wydale has promised me. I'm not allowed to stay up late at parties at home, nor do I wear such pretty frocks.'

'Well, as soon as you're back, I shall arrange one especially for you, and you shall stay up to the very end, how about that?'

Sarah's face cleared. 'Then I shall come home with you. I've promised I shall be a good girl and be nice to his friends when they come. So we must wait until after that, because I have given my promise, and you always tell me that it is naughty to break one's word.'

Eliza though it best to ignore that statement and deftly changed the subject. 'Do you drive yourself round the park, Sarah?'

'I wouldn't do that; I would be scared by myself. Jane always comes with me. There's just room for the two of us in the cart. It's such fun and I've even made Bubbles canter.'

'Did you ask to go out, or did someone tell you when it was available?'

She could see that her sister was becoming bored by this constant questioning. 'I don't know. I think Jane said we should go out for a

175

drive and so we did. The pony and trap was outside waiting for us when we came down.'

Eliza was shocked at how quickly Sarah had adjusted to a completely different routine, living contentedly somewhere that wasn't her home. She had always thought that she would be unhappy away from familiar things, but obviously she was not like a normal five-year-old. She might have limited intellectual capacity, but her sister was obviously developing a certain amount of independence and ability to function away from her family.

'I think I should like to go out for a drive very early tomorrow morning, before the sun is up. Do you think that would be something you'd like as well?'

'Yes I would, I should love to drive you. Shall we go round to the stables and speak to Jethro to make sure that Bubbles will be ready so early in the day?'

Eliza was relieved that Sarah didn't ask why they needed to go out at sunrise; she appeared to accept the strange fact without concern and had suggested herself that they go and speak to a groom. It would be far easier to talk to one of the stable boys when she had Sarah beside her.

For some reason her sister was not viewed with the disfavour that she was. Lord Wydale had obviously circulated some malicious rumour, but she was not going to enquire too closely exactly what he'd said. She already had a shrewd idea.

Sarah led the way round to the back of the house pointing out various aspects as they passed. Eliza learnt that the head gardener kept his tools in a small stone building and that the handsome building held farm carts and carriages. She also learnt that two cart horses were stabled with the carriage and riding horses. She noted that the yard was well kept, the horses, that were not turned out, all looked eagerly over their stalls.

'Which one is Bubbles? If he's a little pony, he won't be able to see out of one of these big stalls, will he, Sarah?'

'You're silly, Liza, he lives in the paddock at the back and he has two goats and another horse for company.'

Eliza noticed that there was a gravelled path leading round the side of the stable block and it was this that Sarah took. The path widened to a larger space in which there was a five-bar gate. Her sister ran across, calling to the small dapple grey pony that was grazing halfway down the meadow.

Immediately the animal raised his head and with pricked ears trotted briskly over to greet his new friend. 'I have nothing for you now,

Bubbles. But I have bought my very best sister, Liza, to meet you. You shall take us both for a drive tomorrow morning.'

Eliza walked across and joined her sister as she hung over the gate to stroke the animal. He was far smaller than she'd hoped, too small to pull a trap with two healthy females in it any great distance. Her plan to escape the next morning seemed doomed before she'd even finished arranging the details.

'Look, Liza, here comes Silky. She's the horse that the housekeeper, Mrs David, uses when she goes to market. There's a bigger cart for Silky and it's kept next to the one that Bubble uses.'

'Silky's a lovely horse. I wonder if we could ask to use him instead of Bubbles tomorrow? You see, darling, I am such a very large lady, I doubt if Bubbles could pull us very far before being completely worn out.'

Sarah looked from the pony, no more than twelve hands high, to her sister, almost six feet in her stockings. 'Yes, I think that might be best. I'm sure Jethro, the nice groom who looks after Bubbles and Silky will do that. Shall I go and ask him straightaway?'

Eliza nodded. If they could have use of the larger cart it would be possible to take Ann and Jane with them. Although she was prepared to leave with only Sarah, she would much prefer them all to be well away from wherever it was they were, before Lord Wydale and his gentlemen friends arrived tomorrow afternoon.

She strolled after her sister and, when she arrived back in the stable yard, Sarah was deep in conversation with an oldish man, who was nodding and smiling as he answered. Eliza tried to look unconcerned as she walked across to join them.

'Good afternoon, Jethro. I am so sorry to burden you with my problems so soon after arriving here, but Sarah is determined to show me how well she drives around and as you can see, I'm far too large to be pulled around in her little cart.'

She waited for the speculative gleam to appear in the older man's eyes, for the sneer, the sly looks that all the inside staff had been giving her. The man merely nodded, his face open and polite.

'It'll be a pleasure, miss. When I heard that Miss Sarah's sister was coming to stay I was that relieved. She's not really up to all this, is she, miss?'

'You're quite correct, Jethro. I'm afraid she's not as other young women of her age, and does need to be carefully looked after.' She hesitated, not sure if she should reveal any more of her fears.

The groom pre-empted her. 'You might not remember me, Miss Fox, but I worked for Captain Carruthers, the young man you were to marry, before he was killed fighting for his king and country. I don't believe a word of the nonsense that I've been hearing. Lord Wydale is up to something, that I'm certain.'

The man stopped guiltily, and glanced around in case he had been overheard. Sarah had wandered off to play with a cat and a litter of kittens which were living in an empty box in the far corner of the yard. It was safe for them to resume their conversation.

'Winterton House used to belong to an elderly lady, Miss Simpkins. I believe she was Lord Wydale's great aunt. She was a good employer and I have been happy here these past five years, but when her great-nephew arrived a few months ago to take possession, I decided it was time to look for another job. I didn't like the cut of his cloth, if you take my meaning miss.'

'But you're still here, Jethro, did something happen to change your mind?'

'Yes, Miss Fox, it did. Lord Wydale decided to rent out the property and farms to a family from London. They have been here ever since, but Lord Debden heard his father had suffered an apoplexy and decided it was time to return to Northumberland. So he took his

180

family away with him two weeks back.'

Eliza smiled warmly at the man. 'Thank God, he did, Jethro. You being here, and knowing me to be nothing to do with Lord Wydale and his coterie, might very well be the lifeline I've been praying for. I need to get us away from Winterton House before his lordship arrives tomorrow afternoon. Once seen in his company my good name will be gone forever. No matter what I say or do, I shall be always tainted by association.'

'I thought as much. You get your maids and bags down here at dawn, and I shall do the rest. It's not far from here to Newfield, and there's an overnight mail calls in at eight o'clock every morning. I'll get you all there in time to catch that, never fear.'

Abruptly the man turned away and vanished inside a loose box. Eliza realized they were being spied on; a surly-looking individual, wearing a red-spotted neckerchief and rough brown coat, had just come in to the yard leading one of the large shire horses Sarah had told her about.

She decided it was time to return to the house; it was almost five o'clock and she felt sure that Sarah would soon be demanding supper. She wished she knew how long the eavesdropper had been lurking there. Had he heard Jethro offer to help them escape the next morning?

She glanced back and was met with a stare of such malevolence that she flinched and hurried on. Whoever the unpleasant ruffian was, he was no friend of hers.

14

The small party was ready at dawn. Eliza had told Sarah of their clandestine departure and, as her sister had never driven out before sunrise, she thought the escapade exciting.

'Miss Fox, I have the bags packed, and am just waiting for Jane to arrive with Miss Sarah's doll. She left it behind in her bedroom and as you know she will not travel without it.'

Eliza had decided that they should make good their escape via the servants' stairs. They were less likely to be seen if they went that way. Sarah waited impatiently for Jane to join them. They had convinced her it was an elaborate game of hide and go seek and that they were trying to get to the stable without being spotted by the housekeeper.

Jane arrived her face creased with worry. 'We're too late, miss. There's chambermaids about already. You can't go down the back stairs now.'

'In which case you go down that way. Miss Sarah and I will use the main stairs. If we're accosted I shall tell them the truth: that Miss Sarah wishes to see the sunrise over the house and that we're taking out the horse and trap in order to do so. Don't bring the bags in case you meet anyone. Put them in my closet where they won't be seen.'

The two maids did as instructed and Eliza called Sarah over to her. 'We're going to go down the main stairs. Jane says no one wants to play hide and go seek today because they're all too busy. Are you ready for your adventure?'

'I am. I've never been up when it's not light. Do you think that we'll be in time to see the sun come up?'

Eliza waited to reassure her sister, that they would be in plenty of time, until they were both visible and audible. It would do no harm for any hidden listeners to hear them discussing the reason they were leaving the house at such an early hour.

She knew that the side door would be the easiest to open for it had only two bolts and no key to turn. She expected to be accosted at any moment. Her hands were shaking as she struggled with the door.

'Can I help? I'm a very strong girl.' Sarah added her weight and the bolts slid back silently.

They stepped out into the greyness and found the two girls waiting for them anxiously. Eliza signalled that they should proceed in silence. They walked down the length of the house and took the path that led to the coach house and stables. There were already sounds of clattering buckets and stamping hoofs which indicated at least one other groom was working.

They crept quietly past the yard all walking on the grass in order to avoid the sound of crunching gravel. To her extreme relief Jethro was waiting with the horse and trap. He nodded a greeting but his smile was absent. They scrambled inside and Jethro jumped onto the box, gathered up the reins, released the brake and they were moving.

No one spoke until they were away from the house; even Sarah was subdued. Eliza felt her pulse slowing and she began to believe they had made good their escape.

'Jethro, I think it would be better if you didn't drive us to the village. You said it was no more than a mile or two across the fields to the inn so we shall walk.' She had decided during the long sleepless night that she would tell Sarah they were going to London to see the menagerie at the Tower. She knew that her sister had always wanted to visit the sights and this should be enough to persuade her to get on the mail coach without making a fuss.

'Very well, Miss Fox. I'll take the carriage through the woods and around the lake. If anyone is watching I doubt they'll be able to see that the vehicle is empty.'

Eliza thought this an excellent idea. 'If you wait there for an hour and then return at a canter as though you're worried about our continued absence. Tell the housekeeper that Miss Sarah wanted to explore and asked you to wait, but we never returned. That way you should be above suspicion when our disappearance is discovered.'

She glanced at her sister, waiting for Sarah to comment on the change of plans, but she was asleep, her face hidden inside her fashionable chip straw bonnet. She checked that both Jane and Ann understood and they nodded.

The carriage bowled along through the trees, the dawn chorus filling the air, but this morning Eliza didn't hear it. She flinched and jumped at every shadow convinced that they were being followed by sinister, dark-cloaked figures. She knew she was being fanciful, but until they were safely travelling towards London in the company of others she would not believe they were safe.

Twenty minutes after leaving the stables Jethro pulled up. He turned round on the box. 'Take the path over there, Miss Fox. You'll come to a stile after a bit, climb over and take the path through the fields. You'll be able to see the church spire so you can't get lost. The White Hart is next to the church.' He touched his cap. 'Good luck and God speed.' He didn't get down to help them dismount knowing it would take valuable time.

Eliza watched the only friend she had at Winterton House vanish between the overhanging trees. Now she was on her own. It was up to her to get them all safely away before Lord Wydale appeared that afternoon with his disreputable friends and their ladybirds.

'Come along, we have to take this little track. Sarah, why don't you and Jane run on ahead and see if you can find the stile we have to climb?'

She waited until they were out of earshot before speaking to Ann. 'We have ample time to reach the inn. I'm hoping there will be a private parlour we can use; I expect Sarah will be ravenous and demanding breakfast by then.'

'Miss Sarah doesn't seem bothered about the change of plans. She's not accustomed to being up so early so I reckon she'll sleep as soon as we're on the mail coach.'

'I shall tell the innkeeper the same story. If he enquires about reserving seats for the return journey I shall explain that we are unsure exactly when we wish to come back. You must talk about the Tower and all the exciting things we intend to see. That way I hope we will not appear suspicious.'

She heard Sarah running back laughing and calling far too loudly, 'Liza, Liza, we have found it. It's just a little way ahead.'

'Good girl. Are you looking forward to going to London and seeing the animals at the Tower?'

For a moment Sarah looked bewildered. 'Are we going to London? I had forgotten that. I love animals. Shall we have cakes as well?'

'Of course we shall. We have to travel for quite a way on the coach before we get to London, but you like to travel in a coach, don't you, darling?'

Sarah smiled happily. 'Shall I get to sit by the window?'

'I'm not sure, my dear, it rather depends how many other passengers there are already travelling, but if there's a space be sure it shall be yours.'

★ ★ ★

The walk across the fields was accomplished in less than an hour, but was sufficient time for the sun to have risen and the villagers to be about their business. Eliza was pleased that their route took them behind the High Street and directly into the inn yard.

Thankfully this was deserted. The ostlers were not needed to change the horses for at least another two hours. 'Let's go inside and find some breakfast, I'm sure everyone is hungry after that long walk.' Eliza could have added hot and dirty but wisely refrained. If Sarah thought she was untidy she would demand to go back and change her garments.

Inside, the flagged hallway was well scrubbed and the welcoming smell of freshly baking bread greeted them. Eliza spotted a small brass bell on a side table and rang it loudly.

The landlady appeared wiping her floury hands on a clean white apron. 'Good morning, miss. You're a mite early for the stage, but I expects you'll be wanting a nice breakfast before you travel.'

'Yes, thank you, that's exactly what we would like. We want four seats on the eight o'clock mail coach. We're going to Town to see the Tower.' Eliza smiled brightly, wishing she had not been so voluble.

'And a nice day you have for it, miss. It's only two hours to London so you'll have plenty of time to look round before having to come back.'

The landlady ushered them into a snug room which had a cheerful fire crackling in the grate. 'I'm so hot, Liza,' Sarah whined, 'I don't want to sit in here with a fire going.'

'I shall open the window, Miss Sarah, and then you can sit by it. You'll hardly notice that there's a fire at all.'

Eliza smiled her thanks at Jane. She was too on edge to deal with Sarah's tantrums at the moment. She realized that they hadn't been asked what they required for their breakfast, she was about to ring the bell again but thought better of it. In her present mood it would be wise to present her sister with food rather than give her the option of demanding something that was unavailable.

A loud thump on the door heralded the arrival of their meal. A surly youth staggered in carrying a laden tray. He slammed it down on the dark oak table that ran across the far end of the room. He didn't offer to lay up the table or unload but tugged his greasy forelock and stamped back from whence he'd come.

'Well I never! I hope the food is better than his manners,' Ann said, as she hurried over to set out the meal.

This display had restored Sarah's good humour. 'Wasn't he a naughty boy, Liza? Look, see how he's spilt the milk on the tray.'

Eliza walked over to join the others. This

display of ill-temper had added to her feeling of disquiet, as though it was an omen. This would not do! She must not allow the incident to unsettle her; she had to keep a sense of perspective and remain cool and calm if their escape was to be successful.

'This looks delicious. What are you going to have, Sarah? I shall have some of this crusty bread and a little of the conserve.'

She watched her companions eat a hearty breakfast, but was unable to swallow more than a mouthful of two herself. The freshly baked bread turned to solid lumps in her mouth and the sweetness of the strawberry jam made her feel nauseous. She managed to drink something from her glass of buttermilk but even this made her gag.

The hands on the mantel clock seemed stationary. Every time she heard a raised male voice or the sound of a horse in the cobbled yard she tensed, waiting to be accosted and forced back to Winterton House. She knew she would do anything to avoid being part of an unpleasant scene. Their appearance so early in the morning on foot was already, she was sure, giving rise to gossip.

They were strangers in the village and the staff at the country inn would be speculating about them and trying to decide from which house they had come. She began to wish she had not tried to organize this on her own, but had sent for Edmund instead of banishing him from the house.

By the time they had all visited the privy and tidied themselves, there was an air of expectancy in the building. The yard was bustling with ostlers whose job it would be to change the horses and have the mail coach ready to leave in less than ten minutes.

At last! Eliza gathered up her reticule and gloves and checked that her bonnet was securely tied before turning to the others. 'I do believe it's time for us to go outside. We have only a few minutes to scramble aboard and must be ready and waiting when the coach arrives.'

They stood huddled against the wall beside the other two passengers. Eliza eyed them surreptitiously, checking that they were not from Winterton and in the employ of Lord Wydale. The two men were dressed in country garb, stout boots, heavy britches and cloth coats. The younger of the two became aware of her inspection and his face split in a friendly grin.

'Good mornin', madam. Off to see the sights? Me dad and me — '

His father interrupted him. 'Hush up, lad. Don't be bothering the lady.' The young man turned an unbecoming shade of red and dropped his head in embarrassment at the public reprimand.

Eliza was about to offer him some comfort when she heard the sound of the coach arriving and the moment passed. It had barely rocked to a halt before the door was flung open by an ostler.

'Anyone getting off here?' There was a mumbled sound of voices from inside but nobody emerged. The man turned to Eliza. 'There's only two seats inside, miss. Your girls will have to travel on the top.'

Eliza stared with horror at the seats on the roof of the coach. She couldn't ask Jane or Ann to travel in such a precarious fashion. She would have to leave them behind, and they could take the next available spaces and make their own way to Mr Reed's home in Grosvenor Square.

Quickly she delved into her bag and withdrew some coins. 'Here, Jane, take these; they will be enough to see you to your destination. Sarah and I will travel on this vehicle you must wait for the next.'

The look of profound relief on both women's faces told her she had made the right decision. 'Quickly, Sarah, in you get. See, there are two seats on the side and one of them is by the window just as you wished.'

Allowing her sister no time to argue she

bundled her inside and no sooner had they squeezed into their allotted places than the door slammed, the steps were removed, and the coach lurched away. She had done it. They were on their way. There was nothing Lord Wydale could do now to prevent their escape. She knew that they would halt for a final change of horses but none of the passengers would be asked to alight. With a sigh of relief she settled back and prepared herself for the barrage of questions she believed Sarah would have.

15

Eliza risked a glance around the confined space of the coach, not wishing to draw attention to herself but curious about her fellow travellers. The four passengers facing her were all asleep so she was free to stare as rudely as she wished.

In the far corner was a soldier in scarlet regimentals, his long booted feet jammed into the corner, his face hidden by the brim of his shako. Next to him were two ladies of indeterminate age, one of them obviously the mistress, the other the companion. The last space was occupied by a burly farmer who hadn't bothered to scrape the farmyard dung from his boots before he left.

Her nostrils curled in distaste as the pungent aroma wafted across to her. Sarah was bound to comment and she braced herself for further embarrassment. She turned to speak to her sister but she had fallen instantly asleep. The early rise and rocking motion had acted like a lullaby.

Gently she slipped her folded cloak between Sarah's head and the hard wooden frame of the coach. Satisfied she had made her as comfortable as possible, Eliza slipped her reticule in between them not wishing to doze off leaving it accessible to the other passengers. She could not afford to lose the money she had with her for their journey.

The elderly woman she had sat next to was eating some kind of meat pasty with obvious relish. The smacking of lips and slurping were clearly audible in the almost silent interior. Eliza had noticed that the last passenger, squashed into the corner, was a young curate who had fallen asleep with his Bible resting open on his lap.

There was nothing she could do until they reached London. They were safe. She had achieved her objective. Gradually her eyes closed and soon she was dozing like the rest of the occupants. She didn't wake until the coach rattled into its final halt where the ostlers were waiting to make a rapid change of horses.

Sarah sat up rubbing her eyes looking round in surprise as if unsure where she was. 'Are we there? Do we get out here, Liza?'

'No, they are changing the horses, we still have a little way to go yet.' She noticed that all the passengers were sleepily sitting up and attempting to ease the cramps and stiffness from their limbs. She felt the vehicle rock as someone climbed down from the roof.

The shouting and clatter in the cobbled yard as the new team were backed into place told her they were almost ready to depart. Then she heard raised voices and the coach door was flung open.

'Miss Fox, Miss Sarah, I do believe you have forgotten I was to meet you here.'

Eliza felt her colour fade as she stared into the blackness of Lord Wydale's eyes. Instinctively she shrunk back against the seat unable to reply coherently. If she asked the soldier to help would he do so?

Then she felt her sister scramble forward greeting him like a close friend. 'Lord Wydale, I am so glad to see you. This is a bumpy and uncomfortable coach I should much prefer to ride in yours.'

Before Eliza could protest, her sister was being handed down the steps. She had no choice, she had to follow. Hastily gathering together their possessions she jumped down to see her sister vanishing into the busy coaching inn.

So near to London it was possible that there would be people inside who would recognize Wydale and seeing a lovely young, unescorted lady on his arm would draw their own conclusions. Gathering up her skirts she ran after them arriving inside just as they were walking up the stairs together.

'Sarah, what do you think you're doing? Come down here at once.' Eliza rarely used this tone when addressing her sister, but when she did, she knew Sarah would respond. The girl snatched her arm away from Wydale's and ran back to stand beside Eliza her face penitent her big blue eyes brimming.

'I'm sorry, Liza. I forgot that I should not go anywhere without you or Jane. Are you cross with me?'

'No, darling, I'm not cross. Here, let me dry your eyes.' She placed her arm protectively around her sister's waist and deliberately turned her back on the saturnine figure approaching. 'I shall endeavour to find a private room for us. I have no wish to stand here.'

'I have bespoken a private parlour, Miss Fox. The room is upstairs, it was there that I was escorting Miss Sarah.'

Eliza refused to turn, to acknowledge the man standing unpleasantly close. So close she could smell him, the heavy perfume he used could not disguise the stink of unwashed male. She tightened her hold on Sarah and her sister knew better than to disobey the unspoken command. If she remained resolute and refused to turn then surely he would go away? But he didn't.

He moved nearer, until he was pressing

into her back. He lowered his head in order to whisper in to her ear. 'If you wish me to drag you upstairs then I shall be happy to oblige. Believe me, madam, no one will ever forget the spectacle I shall create if you do not do as I say without a fuss.'

Bile rose in her throat. Swallowing desperately Eliza stepped sharply sideways and without a word stalked across the vestibule and on to the stairs. Halfway up she realized she had no idea which direction to go when she reached the top. She slowed her place waiting for him to catch up.

'A wise decision, Miss Fox. Our rooms are to the left, the third door.'

Eliza knew she was beaten; somehow he had discovered her plans and with consummate ease had recaptured them both. She was comforted by the thought that she still had the stiletto sewn into her chemise.

She led the way into the suite of rooms they had been allocated and was relieved to find a chambermaid waiting to assist them. At least with a servant present the conversation would remain respectable. Sarah remained at her side still worried about the reprimand she had received earlier.

'We should like to refresh ourselves and remove the grime of the journey.' Eliza addressed the young girl who curtsied but didn't speak, instead she beckoned and ran across to a panelled door. Eliza thought perhaps the maid was mute so smiled and nodded to indicate she understood.

She wasn't sure if Lord Wydale had followed them in but had no intention of looking over her shoulder to check. She knew a gentleman would never enter a lady's rooms but he was no gentleman and would do as he wished.

'Sarah, can you remove your bonnet yourself?' She watched as her sister fumbled with the bow under her chin but made no move to assist her. It was better that she managed such simple tasks herself; it was too easy to do everything for her and even someone with her limited intelligence had to learn to cope.

Eventually the ribbon untied and triumphantly Sarah snatched off her hat. This small success was enough to restore her normal good humour. 'See, Liza, I did it. Shall I put it on the stand?'

'You're a clever girl, darling; very soon you will be able to tie the bow as well.' Eliza pointed to the folded cloaks. 'Could you possibly shake those out and hang them up?' Knowing this was something easily accomplished, she could turn her attention to the chambermaid who was fidgeting anxiously at her side.

'Is something wrong? Are you unable to speak to me?'

The girl, scarcely more than a child, smiled and pointed to her mouth and then shook her head almost dislodging her white cap.

'But you can understand me?' Eliza asked. Again the maid smiled and nodded. She pointed to a smaller door and mimed the actions of washing one's hands. 'Thank you, I wish to use the commode. Is that also in there?' The door was opened ceremoniously and Eliza could see everything they needed was within.

Satisfied that she had made sure the guests were content, the chambermaid vanished through another door and the sound of her footsteps could be clearly heard echoing along a hidden passageway.

A short time later they were both refreshed and returned to the private sitting room. It was empty. Sarah saw the relief on her sister's face and was prompted to ask about it.

'Liza, why are you cross with Lord Wydale? Wasn't it kind of him to lend us his carriage to go to London and see the sights?'

'I'm sorry, Sarah, we're no longer going to London. His lordship insists that we return to Winterton, that's why I am cross with him.'

'Then I don't like him any more and I want to go home to see Mama.' She looked around noticing for the first time that her companion was missing. Her eyes flooded and large tears rolled down her cheeks. 'I want my Jane, and my dolly. I don't like it here.'

Eliza gathered Sarah into her arms and led her to a comfortable sofa. She was glad that the infatuation for Lord Wydale had evaporated, it would make it so much easier to keep Sarah safe if she didn't want to spend any time with him.

'You must be brave, sweetheart; Edmund and Mr Reed are coming to fetch us very soon. It was naughty of Lord Wydale to take you and now we must do everything we can to keep away from him. You'll not mind missing his party, will you?'

Sarah sniffed loudly and dried her eyes on the skirt of her walking dress. 'When will Jane be here? I don't want to go to parties any more, I want to go home with Jane to see Mama.'

'I know you do, and I promise you we shall all be together again very soon.' Eliza sent a desperate prayer to the Almighty that this might indeed be the case. 'Are you feeling better? I think we had better go downstairs, I don't think Lord Wydale wishes to be kept waiting.'

She sent Sarah back into the bedchamber to collect their bonnets, gloves and cloaks.

Using the mirror above the fireplace she deftly dressed her sister and herself. 'There. Now we're ready to descend. Remember do not speak to him and keep your eyes lowered.'

Lord Wydale was waiting downstairs apparently unbothered by their tardy arrival. 'Miss Fox, Miss Sarah, my carriage is waiting. I shall travel inside with you, I'm sure you understand the necessity for that.'

Eliza ignored him and Sarah, as instructed, kept her head down. The same closed travelling coach pulled by four matched bays was standing at the far side of the busy yard. Gathering up her cloak and gown she sailed across the yard and mounted the steps, at no time raising her head. She hoped that any onlookers would have been unable to recognize either of them enveloped as they were by plain dark cloaks and deep brimmed bonnets.

Assisting her sister into the far corner by the window Eliza sat next to her. She felt the movement of the vehicle as their abductor climbed in, but she kept her head averted, praying silently that he wouldn't choose to sit opposite. She heard the door slam and the carriage rocked again then the driver snapped his whip and they were away, bumping and lurching across the cobbles and out on to the busy toll road.

She forced her breathing to remain even and tried to unknot the muscles in her shoulders. If she could appear outwardly calm and composed then she had won a small victory. She suspected that this man took pleasure from the pain of others.

It was fully half an hour before Wydale broke the silence. 'I believe that your sister is asleep, Miss Fox, so we can talk freely.'

Surprised by his thoughtfulness she turned to look at him and wished she hadn't. His thin lips curved in triumph. 'Where are your two servants?'

'On their way to London by now.'

His hateful chuckle filled the carriage. 'I doubt it, Miss Fox. The eight o'clock mail coach is the only one that leaves that inn. Unless they have walked back to Winterton, they will still be languishing where you left them.'

Eliza stared out of the window, hiding her dismay inside her bonnet. She had hoped that Jane and Ann would be able to go to Fletcher in Grosvenor Square. She refused to give him the pleasure of seeing her discommoded.

'Then I should like to stop at the White Hart and instruct them to come back to Winterton. Will that be possible, my lord?'

'Of course. I would not leave my honoured guests without their staff. I expect you're curious as to how I was able to intercept you so easily?'

Eliza forced her mouth into the semblance of a smile. 'There is no necessity, my lord. I have already realized that the man leading the shire horse yesterday was the driver of the coach that brought me to Winterton.'

Again his laughter washed over her, setting her teeth on edge. 'It's a shame, is it not, Miss Fox, that you were not so observant yesterday?' His face hardened and his eyes glittered dangerously. 'I can assure you that the groom who helped you is very sorry indeed.'

She felt fear immobilize her. She knew what he meant. Poor Jethro had been discovered and punished in some way. She had to know, couldn't help herself from asking. 'You have not harmed him? He had no choice: when I asked him for his assistance he was obliged to agree. He knew me when I was betrothed to Captain Carruthers and felt obligated.'

'Harmed him? My dear Miss Fox, I am no barbarian. He has been dismissed without reference, that is sufficient. He will end in the gutter as he deserves.'

Eliza felt the numbness begin to recede, her breath hissing through her teeth with relief. Then she saw his eyes and knew that he lied. Knew that he had killed the man who'd helped her.

Hastily she looked away — it could prove disastrous if Wydale suspected that she knew how cruel and ruthless he was. He would have nothing to lose and might not wait until his friends arrived that evening to ruin her. She needed to delay matters until rescue arrived.

She felt despair engulf her. There would be no rescue. How could there be? Nobody knew where they were and time was running out.

16

Fletcher watched Jamieson scurry away and wondered if he should have persisted and forced the address of the establishment from the man. The carriage didn't move and he raised his stick to bang again, irritated by the delay.

'Where to, sir? Do you still wish to go to Brooks's?'

Fletcher stared up at the roof of the carriage from which the disembodied voice of his driver spoke to him.

'No, take me home, I have no wish to go anywhere else tonight.'

The carriage rocked forward and, stretching out his long legs, Fletcher rested them on the seat opposite. He didn't want to alarm Wydale by appearing like the wrath of God and demanding to know where he was holding Sarah. That would only exacerbate matters, make what was a private matter common gossip. He could not risk having their confrontation in public. What he intended to do to the bastard was best done away from prying eyes. He had no wish to dance at the end of a rope.

Twenty minutes later the carriage jerked to a halt outside his house. A waiting footman flung open the front door and ran down the steps to open the carriage door. Fletcher didn't wait for the steps to be lowered, but jumped down and strode in to the house. He was going to the study to think. A wry smile curled his mouth as he threw his top coat and hat to the servant. Going to the study to drink was a much more likely option.

He had achieved two of his objectives today — that wasn't bad. Tomorrow he would get the final piece of information from Mayhew. As long as Wydale was around town, Sarah was safe; he had no intention of chasing the man away until he was ready. He patted his pocket, liking the feel of the thick paper document that he had placed there earlier. He had the special licence made out, all he needed to do was find a curate and they could be married anywhere, and any time, that they chose.

He frowned into his brandy glass. He prayed it would not come to such a thing. When he married the love of his life he wished to do it with all the pomp and ceremony she deserved. But, God forbid, he somehow arrived too late and Wydale had violated her, then at least they could be married straight away.

He had only known the Fox family for two weeks, but in that time he had come to think of them as his responsibility. They had replaced the two brothers and mother he had lost all those years ago. After the loneliness of these past few years it would be good to be in the middle of a lively family.

He could not allow himself to doubt that there would be a happy outcome to this situation. Sarah would be returned safely to her family, Eliza would forgive him and Wydale . . . well, he could go to the devil.

★ ★ ★

The next morning he sent out members of his staff to make enquiries amongst the servants of various prestigious houses. If you wanted to know any gossip it was there that you went, not to the master and mistress, they were often the last to know. By lunchtime he was no further forward in his search for information. Sir Percy had vanished from his lodgings in Albemarle Street so couldn't be asked for the address he sought. However, he did know that Wydale and several of his cronies were at a prize fight in the East End and certainly not on their way to wherever Sarah was being held, no doubt Mayhew was amongst those.

Certain that he would not come face-to-face with the villain, Fletcher decided it would be safe to start his own campaign. He intended to speak privately to the men of power within the *ton* and get Wydale's name removed from the lists of members of all the significant clubs in London. He had no intention of telling them the details, he knew that his word would be enough.

Whilst he was achieving his objectives, he also decided to pre-empt Eliza's possible refusal to marry him. He mentioned, in the strictest confidence, to several of the most garrulous of his acquaintances, that he had met a young lady named Miss Eliza Fox, who resided in a small town called Dedham, in Essex, and that he had every intention of making her an offer at the earliest opportunity. He made sure everyone he spoke to knew it would be a love match, that he had set eyes on her and fallen head over ears in love in an instant.

It was after midnight when he eventually returned to his house and his back was sore from congratulatory slaps and his head was spinning from the number of celebratory drinks he had consumed. Somehow a disaster had been turned into a triumph, at least there was no way Eliza could back out now. Word was all over Town they were all but betrothed.

When they got married, either in haste or at leisure, no one would think twice about it. He ran up the stairs and the front door swung open.

Endean bowed deeply. 'Mr Reed, sir, there is a young gentleman waiting to see you. He arrived about an hour ago and, as he was sharp set, we have fed him. Now he is pacing up and down the drawing room like a caged tiger.'

Fletcher was across the vast hall in three bounds. 'Edmund, tell me, has Eliza gone?'

Edmund's face split in to a smile of welcome. 'Thank God, you're here, sir. I arrived about an hour ago and have been most anxious to tell you what happened. Denver and one of my grooms are following the carriage that came to take Eliza to Sarah. Denver will stay, to be on hand if needed, and Roberts will travel post to you here as soon as he knows the location. He will stay with Denver until they are certain neither of them require immediate aid.'

Fletcher embraced the young man. 'Well done, Edmund. Wydale is still in town, so neither Sarah nor Eliza are in any danger from him at the moment. There is nothing we can do tonight, so I suggest we both retire and be ready to leave as soon as we have our direction.'

Fletcher turned and gestured to the butler who was hovering in the background. 'Has a room been prepared for Mr Fox?'

The butler nodded. 'Yes, sir, he has the Green Room. Shall I show you up, Mr Fox?'

Edmund took the candlestick the butler offered him. He smiled wearily. 'I own I am more than a trifle weary, sir. I shall be glad to get my head down.'

★ ★ ★

The next morning the two men were breaking their fast when there was a thunderous hammering on the front door. The breakfast parlour was on the front of the house and overlooked the street. Fletcher crashed back his chair and headed for the entrance hall. It had to be Roberts with the news they wanted.

'Are you ready to leave, Edmund?'

'Yes, sir, my mount will be well rested and I have my pistols in my saddle-bags, primed and ready.'

Fletcher raised an eyebrow; the young man was more mature than he'd given him credit for. 'Good lad, I also shall be armed.'

They met Roberts in the passageway with a footman whose expression indicated his distaste at being obliged to bring a servant through the front of the house.

'Roberts, come with me.' Fletcher escorted the groom down the passageway towards the study. 'We shall convene in here. Come along, Mr Fox, it's better we discuss this between ourselves.'

The groom had the information they had been waiting for. Both Sarah and Eliza were safe and well at the moment at a place called Winterton Hall, near a village named Newfield. It was less than two hours from London.

'Roberts, can you be ready to leave in an hour? Have something to eat and change your garments, I shall provide you with a fresh horse.'

'I'm quite ready, sir. I didn't leave until first light. I had sufficient sleep last night. I shall be more than ready to leave in an hour.'

★ ★ ★

For the remainder of the tedious journey Sarah slept, the excitement and early start proving too much for her frail constitution. Her sister had always retreated into sleep when things became too much. Eliza wished she could do the same, but all she could do was feign unconsciousness and pray that Wydale remained silent on the far side of the carriage.

Eventually the coach began to slow and she realized she could no longer pretend to be oblivious. She straightened, adjusted her bonnet, replaced her gloves and looked out of the window. As she thought, they were just driving down the busy high street of Newfield towards the coaching inn. She glanced across at the dark, silent man opposite.

'Will you permit me to alight here and enquire as to the whereabouts of my maidservants, sir?'

He didn't bother to answer, but rapped sharply on the roof of the carriage and it halted adjacent to the inn. The vehicle rocked as one of the grooms scrambled down and unfastened the door.

'Miss Fox wishes to know if her servants are still within this establishment. If they are tell them to walk back to Winterton Hall immediately.'

She was obviously not going to be allowed out of his sight. Eliza gently shook Sarah awake. 'Sarah, we're almost back at Winterton Hall. Lord Wydale has sent to discover if Jane and Ann are still waiting here for us.'

Sarah sat up, rubbing her eyes and yawning hugely. 'Can Jane travel back in the carriage with us?'

'No, my dear, there is not room for both of

them so it's better that they walk together, don't you think?'

The sound of booted feet on the cobbles was clearly audible and the groom appeared in the open door. 'They was there, my lord, and they're now on their way back to the hall.' The man smirked at Eliza, but she kept her face impassive, it would not do to react to the insolence of these men.

The last few miles back to the hall took longer than she had expected. She realized the roads they had to take were more circuitous than the direct route they had followed that morning, straight across the fields. With any luck they might all arrive at the same time. What she had in mind required all of them to be there.

The carriage halted and Wydale jumped down as soon as the door was open, leaving them to follow as they would. He knew they had nowhere else to go but inside. By the time Eliza had organized Sarah and collected their cloaks, he had disappeared. The front door was opened by the housekeeper.

'I shall have trays sent up to you, Miss Fox, and there will be hot water coming up directly.'

Eliza looked at the woman in surprise; she had not expected such kindness from someone who regarded her as little better than a courtesan. Had there been a change of heart? Had her attempt to escape made the woman realize she was not as she had been described?

The housekeeper went briskly up the stairs leaving Eliza and Sarah no option but to follow. They arrived outside her rooms and this time the door was opened and they were followed inside.

Mrs David glanced over her shoulder as if worried about eavesdroppers. 'Miss Fox, I believe that I owe you an apology. We were grievously misinformed about your true nature. There's nothing I can do to help you get away from here, but I shall do everything I can to keep you safe whilst you're under this roof. I can assure you that anyone who asks shall know that you were an innocent party to this abduction.'

'Thank you, I don't expect you to put yourselves in jeopardy. Jethro helped me to escape and I fear that something dreadful has happened to him for his involvement. I shall be grateful if you could make discreet enquiries as to his whereabouts. I pray that he was just dismissed without reference. My two maids should be back very soon. Please ensure they come up here immediately, and that they also bring trays of food.'

'Of course, Miss Fox. I said I shall do

everything I can to help you both. Lord Wydale holds our livelihoods in his hands, but I shall not let that stand in the way if I think that either of you are in danger from the visitors who are expected tonight.' She paused as if wishing to select her next words carefully. 'Are you expecting anyone to come to your assistance?'

'Indeed I am. We will have been missed and several gentlemen will be galloping here even as we speak.' Eliza prayed her statement was true. She was relying on her brother and Fletcher to come to their aid, but had no certain knowledge that they had even discovered their whereabouts yet. It was down to her to delay the inevitable as long as possible.

The woman smiled, making her appear far younger and less austere. For the first time she curtsied, and with a brief smile whisked out of the door.

'Sarah, let's go into the bedchamber and take off our outer garments. I'm sure you could do with a nice wash and tidy, I know I could.'

'May I stay in here with you, Liza? I don't want to go to the other rooms on my own. I don't like it here anymore, I want to go home.'

'And so you shall, darling, as soon as it can

be arranged. However, until we do leave we shall all be staying in here together. We shall close the door and keep everyone else out until Edmund and Mr Reed come to take us home.'

Her love for Fletcher had resurfaced. It was impossible to deny her feelings any longer. Even though their predicament was partly his fault she forgave him and prayed that he would have ignored her rejection and be racing to the house to save them. With hindsight she thought she might have overreacted, but she was certain Fletcher would forgive her as she had forgiven him.

Sarah seemed somewhat reassured by this information and obediently trailed into the bedchamber as she was bid. Two chamber-maids appeared with jugs of steaming water and they were shortly followed by two maids carrying trays laden with enough food and drink to feed a large family for several days. Mrs David had obviously anticipated her plan to barricade themselves into the bedchamber until help arrived.

All they needed now was for Jane and Ann to arrive and then they could begin to push the furniture across the doors, close the shutters, and make themselves secure from attack. She was relieved to find that there were two empty commodes and a pail with a lid — so their bodily functions were provided for. They had enough food and drink to last them for two days at least, but until all of them were safely inside Eliza could not begin to make her apartment safe. She could see her sister becoming anxious and upset long before Jane arrived.

'Sarah, darling, why don't you find our bags in the bottom of the closet and hang up all our garments? They must be sadly creased after being left down there all day.'

There was nothing Sarah liked better than to busy herself with such mundane tasks and with luck this would occupy her until Jane appeared.

Sarah had just placed the final dress, a dark blue serviceable cotton belonging to Ann, when the door in the dressing room burst open and the two women, red-faced and breathless, appeared.

'Lawks a mercy, Miss Fox, we're that tired, we ran most of the way back.'

Sarah squealed with delight and flung herself into Jane's open arms, needing all the reassurance her beloved companion could give. Eliza, forgetting protocol, embraced her own abigail warmly.

'Ann, I'm so glad you're both here safely. No, don't ask me what happened, I shall tell you all as soon as we have completed blockading ourselves in. We have enough sustenance here to keep us for two days, but I doubt it will be that long before Mr Reed and Mr Fox arrive to rescue us.'

The two women needed no further urging. They understood instantly that it was imperative to keep Lord Wydale and his friends out of these rooms.

Ann pulled the servant's door in the dressing room flush to the wall allowing Jane to ram home the two iron bolts. 'It's a good thing someone decided to put these on this door; we don't have locks on the doors like this at Grove House.'

'No, we don't. Do you think we need to push a set of drawers in front of the opening, just to be on the safe side?'

Jane shook her head. 'No, the passageway is so narrow only one man could try and break open the door; there is no room for a second to help him.'

Sarah was looking bewildered by all this unaccustomed activity.

'Sarah, why don't you take one of these trays into the sitting room and lay out a lovely meal for all of us? The housekeeper has supplied pretty napkins and a matching tablecloth.'

This was another thing Sarah enjoyed doing. Arranging a tea party using real food, crockery and cutlery made it even more exciting. She looked at the two trays with some surprise.

'We don't need both of these, do we, Liza? There's enough food here for lots and lots of people.'

'You're right. You choose which one to take whilst we start work.'

Sarah carefully picked up the smaller tray and carried it into the sitting room placing it on the central, circular table. She looked around and spotted four elegant Chippendale chairs for them to sit on. Satisfied her sister would be occupied for some time, Eliza turned her attention to the more difficult task, that of barricading themselves in safely.

'I thought that the daybed could go across the main door, and then the bookcase and books on top of that, I defy any man, or men, to break open the door with all that in front of them.'

She knew it would be disastrous if they banged on the wooden boards or crashed against the walls with any of the furniture. She had no wish to alert his lordship, or any of his personal retainers. She had no idea where he was, whether he was even in the house or still in the stables. She could not risk him arriving before they were ready.

Twenty minutes later the main door was

safely blocked but she still had to find and secure the servant's entrance which was going to be more difficult as it opened inwards.

'Jane, where was the servant's entrance in Sarah's sitting room? I believe that these rooms are identical to the ones she occupied.'

Jane smiled broadly. 'Over in the corner, miss, just by the shutter. Do you see where the stripes on the wallpaper don't quite match?'

Eliza looked where she was pointing. 'Excellent. I'm not sure how we shall manage with this one, but let me think. Please, could you close the shutters and draw the curtains, I don't want anyone clambering in through the windows.' Jane walked over and pulled the shutter out.

Eliza exclaimed in delight. 'I have the solution. If we leave the shutter as it is, against the wall we can stack furniture in front of it. I believe that will be enough to prevent anyone getting in.'

By the time the three women had finished the only furniture that remained for their use was the circular table and the four chairs; everything else was pushed up against the two entrances.

Eliza looked round, convinced she'd thwarted her captor, at least for the moment. The only point of vulnerability was where the shutter would not close across the window. They had stretched the second one out and with both curtains drawn, and two armchairs piled one on top of the other in the space, she really thought that they would be safe.

'I think we've finished here, thank you both so much. It's a good thing there's no balcony because the only way in will be from the top of a ladder. I doubt that one man, so precariously balanced, could break through our barricade even where the shutter is missing.'

Sarah had helped Jane light the two oil lamps and several candelabra for although it was still early afternoon the room was almost black. The shutters and the heavy curtains shut out not only the sunlight, but muffled the sound from outside.

Eliza frowned when she realized that she wouldn't be able to hear Fletcher arriving. She hoped this would not be an obstacle to his success; she was convinced that all they had to do now was remain calm until rescue arrived.

'Well, Miss Sarah, is the food ready? I declare I'm starving; it's a very long time since I had my breakfast.'

Sarah giggled. 'Yes, it's all ready, but I think you had all better go and wash your faces and hands. You're very dusty and dirty and it's not polite to come to the table like that.'

Eliza stared into the mantel mirror and, by the light of the flickering candles, could see that her face was indeed smudged beyond redemption. She noticed that Jane's hair had parted company with her cap and was hanging in disarray around her shoulders; her face was also streaked with grime and cobwebs.

Eliza smiled at her reflection and turned to the others. 'Come along, we had better do as we've been bid. The water will still be warm in the dressing room. We've achieved our aims. We shall be quite safe in here until help comes.'

17

Eliza doubted that Sarah understood why they were all cooped up in a darkened room in the middle of the day. Everyone was going to have to devote a lot of attention to her if their incarceration was not to be made unbearable.

After eating a hearty lunch Jane and Sarah cleared the table and took the tray back into the cooler dressing room. Whilst they were busy Ann spoke, her face concerned.

'I didn't like to say anything, miss, whilst Miss Sarah was in the room, but just come and look out the window. There's something going on. There's dozens of men out there.'

Eliza hurried across; her abigail stepped aside to allow her to wedge herself between the corner of the room and the two pieces of furniture then press her face into the small gap.

Ann was quite right, there was unusual activity in the grounds. It looked like all the male staff, including some of the footmen, were looking for something. She couldn't hear what they were shouting and didn't dare to move the furniture and open the window in order to listen more closely.

'Yes, there's something going on. We shall have to wait until we get a second message under the door from Mrs Turner. She told us Jethro has disappeared — I think they must be searching for him.' Her voice trailed away and she knew with a sickening certainty what the men outside were really doing. They were looking for a corpse. She didn't need to see any more. Jethro was dead, murdered by that odious monster who had intimated as much in the carriage.

She moved away from the window like an old woman, knowing that the groom would still be alive if he had not offered to help them. His death was on her conscience. She tottered back to the table. Collapsing on to one of the chairs she dropped her head into her hands with a sob of despair.

How had it come to this? Three days ago she had been so happy — about to announce her engagement to a man she had recognized as being her soulmate the minute she'd set eyes on him.

Now her life was in ashes. Whatever happened next, nothing would bring poor Jethro back to life. She knew she was grieving before her fears had been confirmed, but Wydale's eyes had told her what had happened. It was only a matter of time before the men searching the ground would come across his body.

If their captor was prepared to murder someone whose only crime had been to offer assistance, then what hope was there for the rest of them? Eliza looked around the room, it seemed safe enough, but she knew that somehow that monster would get to them. Where were Fletcher and Edmund? Why didn't they come?

'We must pray together, Ann; pray that Mr Reed and Mr Fox arrive before Lord Wydale comes to fetch me.'

★ ★ ★

Fletcher turned to Edmund. 'I intend to marry Eliza, whatever happens, I have a special licence in my pocket.'

'There will be no need to use that, Mr Reed. Both my sisters will come out of this safe and sound; then you and Eliza can have the wedding that she always dreamed of. I shall march down the aisle with my sister on my arm in front of all our friends and family.'

'God willing! I have sent a note to my man, who is waiting to hear from me at my estate, Hendon Manor. Looking at the map, I estimate that Winterton Hall is no more than ten miles from my home. I have asked Sam to bring two of my men and join us at Newfield. I have also asked for my coachman to bring a closed carriage to transport the ladies.'

'How far is it from London to your estate, sir? If we are leaving within the hour, surely your man will not be able to join us in time?'

'Never fear, Edmund, I have already sent a groom, if he gallops all the way he should be there not long after we leave here. They should be able to cover the miles easily and join us before dark.'

★ ★ ★

The three men clattered out on to the cobbles of Grosvenor Square in slightly more than the hour. All carried pistols in their saddle-bags. Fletcher was confident all eventualities had been covered. The route he had devised would take them across country, and through quieter lanes as he had no wish to draw attention to themselves. Wydale might have spies positioned, watching for him.

It was about two o'clock when they arrived, hot and dusty at the White Hart. To all intents and purposes they were two gentlemen travelling together, accompanied by a male servant. Fletcher dismounted and tossed the reins of his sweating horse to a waiting ostler.

'See to our mounts; we intend to rest here before continuing our journey.'

The man nodded and touched his forelock before raising his hand to take the reins of Edmund's mount. Roberts followed, leading his own horse. He had instructions to pick up any gossip from the men who worked at the inn.

Inside it was cool and dark and appeared deserted. Fletcher looked around and seeing no one he raised his voice and shouted for attention.

He heard the sound of hurrying footsteps and a jovial red-faced man appeared. 'Good afternoon, sirs, can I be of assistance?'

'Yes, my good man. We require a room in which to remove the grime of our journey and whatever food you can provide at this time of day.'

'At once, sir. I shall send one of my girls to conduct you to a chamber. Do you wish to eat downstairs or shall I have a tray sent up?'

Fletcher pondered for a moment, it would probably be best to remain out of sight as long as possible. 'Send up a tray; anything will do, bread and cheese, mutton pie, whatever you have available.'

The man disappeared and moments later a young woman, in cap and fairly clean white apron, appeared. 'Come this way, sirs, we have a room ready.'

The chamber they were conducted to was on the front of the building, overlooking the deserted yard. Fletcher scarcely noticed the polished furniture and sparkling windows. He had more important matters to consider. 'What arrangements have you made to meet Denver?'

Edmund, who had been gazing out of the window, turned to face him. 'He's staying at the next village; it didn't seem wise to be here, so close to Winterton Hall. The presence of a stranger might have caused remark amongst the locals. We're to ride over to the Red Lion and rendezvous at four o'clock.'

'Excellent, the horses should be rested and ready to continue by then. Is it far?'

'No, two miles, but I'd better warn you, sir, the establishment he's using is not half as grand as this. Not somewhere you'd choose to stay.'

Fletcher chuckled. 'Your man Denver sounds a stout fellow. Having a manservant one can trust is invaluable in circumstances like these.'

Edmund looked at him with some surprise. 'I had no idea you had been embroiled in abductions and such things on a regular basis, sir.'

'I haven't, you nincompoop. And stop calling me *sir*, for God's sake. I think, as we're going to become brothers, sooner rather than later, it would be acceptable for you to use my given name.'

The young man grinned, apparently pleased to be accepted as his equal. Edmund turned back at the sound of voices and the clatter of hoofs in the yard, curious to know who was arriving. His face blanched when he saw who dismounted. 'It's Denver. He would only come here in an emergency.' He was about to rush from the room but Fletcher restrained him.

'Hold on, lad, your man will find us soon enough.' He watched, as the same ostler who had dealt with them appeared to take the reins of Denver's hack. He saw them exchange a few words and then the two men walked together into the stables.

'I think your valet has gone to speak to Roberts. It will seem less conspicuous if he comes up to speak to us. I'm sure we shall hear the news soon enough.'

A soft knock at the door caused them both to swing round.

'Come in,' Fletcher barked.

The door opened and a maid staggered in carrying a laden tray followed by the pot-boy who had served Eliza and Sarah that morning. The youth placed the two jugs of frothing porter on the table next to the tray.

'Thank you, that will be all. We shall serve ourselves.'

The two men ignored the food, they were more concerned with what information might be on its way from the stables. Edmund peered out of the window, but the yard remained empty. Fletcher paced, his face stern, his mind turning over the various possibilities that could have brought Denver out of hiding.

He didn't have long to wait before a second bang on the door announced Roberts wished to be let in.

'Well, what's the news? Why has Denver ridden over here instead of waiting for us to come to him this afternoon?' Edmund demanded, pre-empting Fletcher, who was about to ask the same question.

'It's grave news, sir, very grave indeed. It seems that Miss Fox, Miss Sarah and the two maidservants managed to escape from Winterton Hall this morning with the help of a groom. He drove them part of the way and then they walked across the fields. Denver had already taken up his position and saw them walk safely to this very inn.'

'Go on, man, what happened next? I take it from your demeanour that the outcome was not a happy one.'

Roberts shook his head. 'No, sir, it wasn't. Somehow their flight was discovered and Lord Wydale was waiting for them when the coach stopped to change horses. It seems they returned here in his carriage, but didn't come in again, just stopped long enough for a message to be given to Ann and Jane to return immediately to the hall.'

Roberts appeared to be having difficulty controlling his emotions. Fletcher watched him, knowing that whatever was coming he was going to like it even less than the news that Eliza had failed in her attempt to escape.

'Well, sir, Denver thought it would be a good idea to go and talk to the groom, find out who he was and suggest that he left the hall at once, and came to join him where he would be safe from reprisals when the girls' disappearance was discovered. He had almost got within hailing distance, when two men emerged from behind the trees and bludgeoned the groom to death in front of his very eyes.'

'The devil take it! How dreadful.' Edmund clutched the back of a chair.

Fletcher was made of sterner stuff. 'Pray continue your story, Roberts. What did Denver do?'

'He could do nothing; there was no point in revealing his presence. The two assassins dragged the corpse into the bushes and then sent the carriage and horse galloping back towards the house as though there had been a mishap.'

'Thank you; go back down and tell Denver to wait in the stables. We shall join him presently. Make sure you get something to eat too — we're all going to need our wits about us before this day's over.'

He waited until Edmund and he were alone again before speaking. 'This is a very bad business, Edmund. Wydale appears to have stepped over the line. He has always been reckless, but I never thought him a cold-blooded killer. We must eat and then ride over to Winterton Hall and pray that we can release the girls before his cronies arrive.'

Neither men had much appetite, but both knew it was imperative they eat or they would not have the energy to fight. They rejoined Denver and Roberts in the stables half an hour later. Fletcher left a message with the friendly landlord that Sam was to follow on to Winterton Hall when he arrived with the coach and two extra men.

The horses had barely had an hour's rest after their strenuous journey and he knew it would be foolish to press them. 'If we go across the fields we shall be visible for miles.

Is there a more private route we can take, Denver?'

'There is, sir; if you follow me, we can take the track I've been using. No one has accosted me, so I'm pretty sure it's safe.'

They left the White Hart in sombre mood. Denver led the group out of town and down a lane thickly grown with overhanging bushes. A mile along he reined in and dismounted to open an ancient gate.

'In here — we have to ride through these woods and it brings us out quite close to the hall.'

They trooped through and Denver carefully closed the gate behind them. They were obliged to ride single file along this track. Denver raised his hand to indicate they should stop.

What now? Fletcher vaulted from his saddle and tossed his reins to Roberts who was riding just behind. He approached quietly. Denver was staring through the tangle of leaves. 'What is it? What can you see?'

'I think they're looking for the groom, Mr Reed. The grounds are swarming with men and some of them are heading this way; if we don't want to be discovered I reckon we'll have to retreat and come back when it's dark. These men might be employed directly by Wydale, or they might

235

be friendly, but I doubt we can take the chance.'

'Can you recognize the two killers among the men?' Fletcher asked.

'No, sir, I can't. I didn't get a good look at their faces, they were both of medium height, stockily built, and roughly dressed, just like the rest of the people we're looking at now.'

Fletcher swore under his breath. Things were becoming more and more complicated. He had hoped to get into the house and remove the girls before the place was overrun by Wydale's friends who would be witnesses to what he intended to do.

'Denver's right, we must go back. I don't think we should return to Newfield; perhaps we can find somewhere not too far away where we can hide and wait until dusk.'

'There's a charcoal burner's hut, in the very heart of this wood, it's not been used for years, but it would be ideal for us.'

It was only after the horses were unsaddled, hobbled and quietly munching on the lush grass that grew in the coppice, that he remembered about Sam.

'Roberts, I think you'd better go back to the White Hart, hang about somewhere inconspicuous, then waylay my men, and the carriage, before they enter the inn.' He scowled, trying to think where he could send the coach to wait until it was needed. He looked across at Denver. 'You know this area better than I, where should I tell my coachman to wait?'

'Tell him to go to the Red Lion in the next village, it's not much of a place, but no one will ask questions, as long as he's prepared to pay for their silence.'

Fletcher turned to Roberts. 'Did you get that? Explain to my coachman where he's to go, then bring Sam and the two men back here.'

He withdrew his hunter from his waistcoat pocket and glanced at the time. It was already four o'clock. The sky was becoming overcast and the clouds getting thicker, with any luck darkness would fall early tonight and then he would be able to begin his assault on Winterton.

18

Eliza, Jane, and Ann took it in turns at the window, hoping to see them bringing Jethro home injured, but still alive. The two who were not watching the park were occupied with entertaining Sarah; they played endless games of hunt the thimble and spillikins until even Sarah was bored with these.

'It's getting awful dark out there, Miss Fox, no point in standing here anymore,' Jane said, mid-afternoon. 'I reckon it'll be dark early tonight; I expect Miss Sarah will be happy to go to bed in an hour or two.'

'Sarah, would you and Jane like to find us something to eat for our supper? Remember we must eat up all the things that will perish first, leave any pies, fruit and bread until tomorrow.'

'I'm not hungry, Liza, I want to go home and see Mama.'

Eliza detected tears in her sister's voice and knew she was trying her best to be brave. 'Never mind, darling, I'm sure we'll all be home safe and sound very soon. Mr Reed and Edmund will be coming to take us back.'

'If we're going home why did you ask me to

hang all the clothes up? Do I need to pack them up again?'

'What a good idea, Miss Sarah. Come along, let's you and I sort out what we need for the night and put the rest back into the bags. We'll want to be ready and not keep Mr Reed or Mr Fox waiting.'

Eliza smiled gratefully. She was the only one who hadn't managed to have a rest during the afternoon. They had been up at dawn and she had hardly slept the night before. She was bone weary and her head ached. 'I think, whilst you both do that, Jane, I shall have a quick doze. I expect you can be very quiet, can't you, Sarah?'

Jane led the girl into the dressing room and closed the door. Eliza kicked off her slippers but left her travelling dress in place. There was no point in getting anything else creased.

She curled up on the pillows and pulled the soft comforter over her ears. Within seconds she was fast asleep and didn't wake until Sarah shook her gently by the shoulder an hour and a half later.

'Liza, Liza, it's time to get up. Look, I'm all ready for bed and you're in my place.'

Eliza felt fresh and surprisingly hungry. 'I am so glad you've woken me; I could do with my supper now.' Quickly scrambling out of bed, she pushed her feet back into her slippers. 'Do you realize, Sarah, that we're going to have to take it in turns to sleep tonight? I think you must all have the first turn because I've just had a lovely long nap. I shall wake one of you in the middle of the night and take your place.'

Sarah giggled, she liked the sound of these unusual arrangements.

Their supper was more or less the same as lunch, but tasty nonetheless. Cook had provided them with bread and cheese, scones and jam, a plum cake and various cuts of meat. There were also fruit pies and biscuits. To drink they had lemonade and buttermilk. Eliza sniffed the jug suspiciously. 'Do you think this is still fresh enough to drink, Jane? It's been sitting around here for several hours.'

'I stood it in a basin of cold water, miss, so I'm certain it's as fresh as it would be coming straight from the pantry. If we finish it off tonight the lemonade will do for tomorrow morning.'

They were all careful not to waste anything. Eliza was relieved to see there was still more than enough for breakfast, and lunch as well. She prayed they would not need it.

'Are you ready for bed now, Sarah? If you go and get in I shall come and say your prayers with you. Do you wish me to tell you a story, too?'

Sarah shook her head. 'No, I'm very tired. I want Jane to lie down with me, then I shall feel safe and cosy in there. Can we draw the curtains round the bed?'

'Excellent idea, then we can move around in the room and not disturb you.'

★ ★ ★

Ann and Eliza retreated to the sitting room and were silent, both lost in their own thoughts, when they were jerked awake by shouts and screeches of feminine laughter coming from the corridor. Eliza rose in horror. It hadn't occurred to her that Wydale's friends would bring their fancy women with them.

The caterwauling and yelling going on outside told her what she could expect if she was forced to go downstairs. She listened to the clatter and raucous laughter as the couples were escorted to their various chambers.

'I'm going to change my gown, have I anything respectable, Ann?'

'Your apricot muslin with the matching spencer has been left hanging in the closet. It seemed a shame to pack it too soon. The creases have fallen out wonderfully; you would hardly know it had been rolled up most of the day. Would you like me to help you change?'

Eliza was about to refuse as she was quite capable of getting out of her gowns on her own. None of her garments had the rows of tiny buttons that required the assistance of a dresser, but this evening she didn't want to be alone and she certainly didn't want to leave Ann by herself in the sitting room just in case someone hammered on the door.

They were obliged to creep past the bed. Eliza was ready to return to her vigil feeling calmer now that she was freshly dressed, her hair brushed until it shone, silk slippers on her feet and her spencer and reticule in her hand.

There was no sound from inside the curtains on the large tester bed. She tiptoed over and peeped through — both Sarah and her companion were sound asleep.

It was now only a little after six, but tonight it was pitch dark. Whilst they had been busy in the dressing room the guests had obviously gone downstairs for dinner. Eliza was sitting quietly when she heard the sound of heavy feet approaching rapidly. There was an angry bang on the external door.

'You are expected downstairs, Miss Fox.

You are already keeping us waiting for our dinner.' Without waiting for her answer, Wydale attempted to open the door. Eliza shuddered, holding her breath, but it didn't budge. The barrier they had erected held firm.

He threw himself against the door swearing vilely and shouting abuse. Eliza didn't answer him; she cowered in the furthest corner, praying he would go away.

After hammering and shouting for a while, it went quiet, then she heard running feet down the passageway. A moment later someone pulled the servant's door open and she saw a shadowy figure behind the heavy furniture that hid the entrance.

It was hard to distinguish who it was, but she thought it must have been one of Wydale's henchmen because he didn't speak, just pushed hard at the wooden barrier and, on finding it wouldn't move, closed the door again. Eliza heard his feet clatter back.

'I think they've gone, miss. Are we safe now?'

'I don't know, Ann, but I doubt it. Lord Wydale will not give up so easily.'

Yes, she heard footsteps approaching and they were coming down the servant's passageway. She braced herself, knowing that the next few minutes would decide whether she was forced to leave the sanctuary of her chambers.

The servant's door swung inwards and this time it was quite clear who was there. Wydale's head and shoulders were clearly visible above the makeshift barricade. A servant was holding an oil lamp behind him sending flickering shadows across his face. Eliza saw his lips curve in the semblance of a smile, but it didn't reassure her.

'Ah well, my dear Miss Fox, I see that you are dressed and ready. As you no doubt are aware, I cannot get in so you must come out to me.'

Eliza steadied her breathing and replied, slowly enunciating each word. 'I have no intention of coming out, we are all safe and well in here and here we intend to stay. Mr Reed and my brother will be upon you very soon, and I should not like to be in your place when they do arrive.'

'Brave words indeed, my dear Miss Fox. However, unless those gallant gentlemen bring an army with them, they shall not get in here.'

Eliza bit back her question, she didn't wish to appear in anyway eager to talk to him. Surely when Fletcher and Edmund arrived the staff would rally to their side? With so many, they could easily overcome this hateful man and his friends.

'Do not look so sanguine, Miss Fox. I have incarcerated the male staff in the wine cellar, and shall release them in the morning; whatever I wish to do tonight, I shall do it unhindered by them.'

She felt as if she had been punched in the chest. She had to ask, she couldn't help herself. 'And the female staff, what of them?'

His snarl of laughter ricocheted up and down the narrow passageway and the small hairs on the nape of her neck rose. It was the laugh of a madman. 'The female staff? Now that is very interesting you should mention them, my dear Miss Fox.' He leant forward and she saw his face; she did not like what was expressed there.

'It's simple, I'm offering you an ultimatum. Either you come down with me, or I shall take one of the girls instead. I have no need to treat them gently — they are disposable items.'

Eliza's eyes widened in horror as she registered the exact meaning of his statement. He was saying that they would use and abuse any one of the girls with no compunction, and that he was not guaranteeing they would survive the experience. She could not let that happen.

'And if I come down, what then?'

'Then you have my word as a gentleman that the girls will remain locked in the servants' hall until tomorrow morning. Now, are you coming?'

'I have already eaten, and have no desire to sit through dinner watching you and your friends. If you will permit me, I shall join you in the drawing room when dinner has finished.'

For a moment she thought he would refuse her suggestion, then he nodded.

'Very well, it is now six o'clock. I shall expect you in the drawing room at seven-thirty.'

He stepped aside and the door swung shut. The room remained full of his evil presence; it was if a miasma hung over them and it took some minutes to dissipate. Eliza stood rigid, watching the door, wondering if it would swing open again and her nemesis would be there hoping to see her collapsed in a shivering heap on the carpet.

Never! Whatever transpired, she would not give in to him. She might be forced to do things against her will, but he would not break her spirit. Inside she would remain pure whatever he did to her body.

The moment stretched to one minute, two minutes, three and then finally she was sure he had gone. Her knees began to buckle beneath her. An arm came around her waist and she was guided to one of the spindly chairs set by the table.

'Here, you sit still a moment, catch your breath, Miss Fox. That man is the devil. You'll not go down, of course; you can't possibly go down. You'll not need to: it's dark now, and Mr Reed and Mr Fox will be here long before you need to go down.'

'I pray that you're correct, Ann, but I fear that you're wrong. Didn't you hear him say that the house was locked and bolted on the inside? If we can make these rooms impregnable, I'm sure it's possible to do the same to the ones on the ground floor. When Mr Fox and Mr Reed arrive they'll be unable to gain an entrance. They'll have to fetch the militia to break down the door and by then it will be too late.'

Eliza sat for a moment trying to restore her composure. Slowly her head cleared and she began to think lucidly. Of course, things might yet be saved. She had a pistol and her stiletto. Wydale would not be expecting her to be armed and certainly not expect her to be prepared to kill in order to save herself.

As she thought about inflicting death she felt her supper threaten to return. There had already been one person killed, that of the poor groom who had done no more than offer his help, and that was her fault. Could she compound this sin, whatever the provocation? She shook her head. Unless someone else's life was threatened she would not use a weapon to save herself. Was it pointless to take either weapon downstairs with her?

'Listen to me, Ann. I might not be able to save myself, but I can save Sarah. When you move the barrier to let me out, the three of you must come as well and slip down to the wine cellar and let the male staff out. Then they can escort you outside and you can wait until help arrives.'

Ann looked at her in astonishment. 'They'll have thought of that, Miss Fox. What's to stop them coming in when we unbolt the door? If they do, then they'll have Miss Sarah as well.'

Eliza understood why he had given in so easily to her demands. 'Stupid of me, of course they will.' She closed her eyes, trying to force her whirling brain to make sense of something that was senseless. 'I know what we must do; they're not expecting me to come out now. If I go at once, I can hide in a room and wait. This way you can all remain safe.'

Eliza picked up her reticule, weighted down by her small pistol, and checked the stiletto was safe in the seam of her chemise. She had no intention of using them, but it gave her a certain sense of security knowing they were there.

She slipped back through the darkened bedchamber. Ann managed to slide back the bolts, but they grated horribly in the silence. Eliza held her breath, had the noise been heard? When they pushed it back the final inch would men thrust their way in and capture them? She pressed her ear to the crack, but could hear nothing. She would have to risk it. Taking an oil-lamp in one hand, her skirt in the other, she waited for her maid to push back the final bolt.

'No, don't. We mustn't open the door like this. If there's anyone waiting outside the light will alert them. We must douse the candle and this lamp before I step into the passageway.'

'How are you going to relight the lamp, miss, you don't have a tinderbox? Just a moment, I'll fetch the one we used. We've plenty of candles, all I've to do is make sure that one is left alight.'

Eliza put the ribbon of her reticule over her wrist and the tinderbox in the same hand. This left the other one to hold her skirts and the oil-lamp. She doubted she could do both successfully.

'I think it would be easier if I took the candlestick as this lamp is too cumbersome.' They swapped the items over and then she was ready. The candlestick was much easier to hold and Eliza waited by the door surprised her hands were not shaking like a blancmange.

'Right. I'm going to blow out my candle. You must turn out the lamp at the same time. Are you ready?'

'Yes. Good luck, miss.'

Immediately the room was plunged into darkness. Eliza pushed open the door and slipped like a wraith out into the passageway. She stepped away from the door and leant against the wall, breathing heavily. She heard the bolts being pushed home and sighed with relief. The first part of her plan had been accomplished.

She was about to use the tinderbox to light the candle when she heard a sound further down the passage. She froze, holding her breath. Was she discovered?

She heard someone scratching and then a man clearing his throat. Good, she was undetected. However, if she attempted to strike the tinderbox whoever it was would be upon her at once. She had no choice, she would have to inch her way in total darkness until she found a door that opened or came to a twist in the corridor. Once around a corner it would be safe to light her candle.

She felt the darkness closing in on her. She was suffocating; there was no air, no light. Her feet refused to move and she knew it could only be a matter of time before the hidden watcher realized he was not alone in the passageway.

19

Paralysed by fear, Eliza leant against the cold wall knowing that the longer she remained there, the more likely it was she would be discovered. She closed her eyes and immediately the blanket of fear lifted a little. If she imagined she was playing a game of blind man's buff, then perhaps she could manage to finger her way along the wall until she was safe.

She stretched out her left hand, pressing it and then took a nervous step sideways. No one shouted at her. No one had heard her tentative movements. Step-by-step she edged along the pitch-dark passageway for what seemed like hours.

Suddenly her hand was waggling about in mid air. Her pulse jumped in excitement. She had found the turn in the corridor that she was seeking. She shuffled back a step until her fingertips gripped the corner then continued on her way, and, like a mountaineer clinging to a mountaintop, she slowly accomplished her goal.

How many yards did she have to go before she could open her eyes and light the candle?

From what distance could the single flame of a candle be seen? She would have to estimate the distance she had travelled from the corner. Not more than two yards she was certain. But had she moved more than this? It felt as though she'd been crabbing her way in the musty darkness for a mile at least, but knew that this couldn't be the case. Perhaps it was only a yard from the edge — it would be too late when she lit the candle as the glow would reveal her lurking presence. She had no wish to be chased down a pitch-dark corridor by an enraged murderer.

Even in her extremity she was forced to half smile at the melodrama. She was behaving like the heroine in a Gothic novel. She didn't know who was hidden or even if he was a murderer. In fact she didn't know that a murder had even taken place. Her vivid imagination had supplied the details; Jethro could be alive and well and drinking a pint of ale in the local village inn.

She felt calmer now, and made her decision. As she didn't know exactly how far she had come, she would edge a further two yards and be certain she was safe. The thought of being able to strike the tinderbox and light a candle, gave her the impetus she needed to speed up her snail-like pace. Still keeping her leading arm extended she almost skipped down the corridor, allowing the wall to take her weight.

Almost far enough. She would take two more steps and then stop and light the candle. But the wall behind her moved and her clutching hand was waving frantically in mid air. It all happened so quickly. One minute she was safe, her back firmly against the wall, the next tumbling backwards down a pitch-dark hole, candle, tinderbox and reticule scattered in all directions. She felt herself spinning over and then a sickening thud as the side of her head hit the wall and everything went black.

★ ★ ★

In the inky blackness, Fletcher heard Denver, who was keeping watch down the path, shout out. Thank God! At last. What could possibly have delayed them for so long? He flicked his horse's reins from around the branch it had been tethered to. All the mounts were tacked and ready to ride. He glanced back down the path. By holding his lantern aloft he was just able to distinguish a similar glow approaching. He decided to go and meet them. There was no need to remain quiet as all self-respecting men would be home eating their dinner. They were unlikely to meet anyone abroad at this time.

The wind had got up and branches were waving wildly above his head; his lantern went out. 'God's teeth! That's all I need!'

Impatiently he swung round and poked the stick from which it hung towards Denver whose lantern was still burning brightly. 'Here, relight this for me and let's hope the wind doesn't blow it out again.'

Without waiting to see that his companions were ready, Fletcher dug in his heels and cantered off down the lane. Riding so fast was a foolhardy exercise in broad daylight and sheer madness in the dark.

'Is that you, Sam? Where the hell have you been? We expected you an hour since.' His voice echoed through the trees. He heard the rattle and thumps as riders approached at speed. Reining in sharply in order to avoid a collision, Fletcher called over, 'What happened, Sam? Where's the coach?'

'I was forced to turn back and wait in a coppice just outside the town for an age, sir. Three carriages appeared on the London Road and headed straight for the White Hart. I expect they were the guests that his lordship was expecting. Until they passed on their way to Winterton there was nothing I could do. I couldn't risk being seen. The town is deserted at night and three men and a closed carriage were bound to be noticed.'

'Where's Roberts? I sent him to give you instructions.'

'We've met nobody. It's dark, so I thought it safe to send the coach on down the tradesman's route. It's waiting in the drive, with lanterns extinguished, of course.'

Edmund pushed his horse closer. 'Did you say my man Roberts, is not with you?'

'No, sir, there's only the three of us.'

'Don't fret, Edmund. I'm sure he's on his way back; he must have had to hide as well and will join us later.'

'But how did you find your way here without Roberts' assistance? Surely you didn't ask the locals for directions?'

Sam laughed. 'Of course I didn't. But I'm an expert at following a trail and the one you left is clear as day even in the dark, if you get my meaning.'

This remark dispelled the tension a little. Fletcher thought rapidly; there was no point in hanging about waiting for the missing groom, hopefully he would have the sense to follow on.

'Come along, gentlemen, we have unfinished business. Denver, you had better lead the way, I'm like to miss the path.' He moved his horse to one side in order to let the other go by.

They had travelled scarcely a mile, bobbing lanterns making pools of golden light above their heads, when they were greeted by a familiar voice.

'Thank God, I thought I'd missed you. I beg your pardon, Mr Reed, Mr Fox, for being gone so long, but it was unavoidable.'

'No need to apologize, Roberts; Sam has explained what happened. I'm glad you're safe. Did you come past the hall on your way here?'

'I did, sir. I wasn't sure if you had already reached the place so dismounted and went to have a look first. The stables are deserted, no grooms, no gardeners, nothing. The boxes are locked and the horses safely inside, but there's no one there. No one alive that is.'

'You found the cadaver?' Fletcher enquired sharply.

'Yes, sir, I did. The poor fellow's stretched out on the floor of a tack room, but no sign of anyone living and another thing, there's not a chink of light shining anywhere. Nothing at all, not even from the servants' quarters. It's like it's like it's closed up and everyone's gone away.'

'In which case, we have no need to remain silent or hide ourselves. Speed is what we need now. I have a bad feeling about this — it's as though we're expected and that bastard has prepared some sort of trap.'

He urged his horse forward resuming his reckless speed and the others had no choice but to follow. They resembled a small group of cavalry as they thundered, in single file, back down the path to erupt in the far corner of the grounds of Winterton Hall. The long grass soon became manicured turf and, riding coat flapping round him like a horseman of the Apocalypse, Fletcher led the way to the rear of the building.

He heaved on the reins and his horse reared back scattering gravel. Vaulting from the saddle, not waiting for the others to catch him up, he led his sweating horse straight into the cobbled stable yard.

'Sam, find the coach and get it here. Billy can take care of the horses.'

'After the noise we made, sir, I reckon Thomas will come on his own.'

Sure enough, by the time the men had removed their pistols from their saddle-bags and loaded them, the sound of wheels, and clinking harness, was clearly audible.

Fletcher waited for the coach to halt before calling out to the coachman. 'Thomas, you come with us — bring your musket. Billy, we're leaving the horses in the yard. See that they're made comfortable and tethered, but

258

don't untack them, we might wish to make a quick exit.'

He turned to the others. 'Keep your lanterns low, hold them down by the ground, just in case anyone happens to look out of the window and sees us approaching.' Fletcher set off at a run, through the arch and around to the rear entrance.

'Right, everybody. No more talking. I want you to be able to hear my instructions and I don't wish to raise my voice.' He swung his lantern round the circle of faces. All six of them nodded. 'Denver, you've been watching this house for the past three days, you'd better try the doors and windows at the front. Take Roberts and Sam with you, and circle the house. It's just possible that something might have been left open.'

'Edmund, let's investigate the back of the building; it's here I think we'll find an entry. It's strange that no one's about. I wonder what happened to the staff tonight? Perhaps they've all been given the night off; it happens when the master wishes to have an evening of debauchery.'

'If they'd been given the evening off, Fletcher, I'm sure Roberts, or your men, would have seen them streaming into the village. No, something more sinister is happening here. I hope to God nobody has been hurt. We have one death on our conscience already.'

Fletcher frowned in the darkness. He had not suspected Edmund was so softhearted; he hoped that when the moment came the boy wouldn't falter. His life might depend upon Edmund's courage.

Holding his lantern beneath his outspread riding coat he explored the back of the house, trying doors and windows, but all were soundly bolted and the interior shutters pulled across. It was as though the occupants were expecting a siege.

As soon as the thought was there he knew it for the truth. Wydale was expecting him and had prepared the house to withstand all but a full attack from the military. A handful of men could not hope to break in.

For a moment he was nonplussed, unable to push a feeling of dread away. 'If we can't get in, then we can't save them from being raped by the group of monsters within.' He scowled, thinking hard, not aware he'd spoken aloud. He turned to Edmund.

'This place is locked up as tight as a drum. We'll not get in the doors or windows, we shall have to think of something else. I'm sure the others had no better luck, but we shall wait on them to return, just to be sure.'

Edmund didn't answer and he thought for

a moment he hadn't heard. He turned and raised his lantern in order to see the young man's face. It was drawn and pale. Cursing under his breath, he realized he must have spoken his thoughts aloud once too often. Edmund was not much more than a boy, how could he expect him to shoulder such responsibility without flinching?

He stepped forward and placed his arm around Edmund's shaking shoulders. 'I'm sorry, lad. I'm sure things are not as black as I said. We shall get in, never fear, and your sisters will emerge unscathed. Now, you have to be strong. You cannot let your imagination run riot.' He felt the trembling still and the young man took several steadying breaths.

'Thank you, Fletcher. I apologize for my weakness, but your words were so graphic, I have been pushing the reality to one side. You merely stated what we both know could be the case.' He stepped away and Fletcher's arm dropped back. 'However, I can hear no screaming, no shouts, no running feet. Even with the shutters drawn I'm sure if something hideous was taking place we should be able to hear it out here.'

'You're right, Edmund. I think we're in time. And I know how we can get in. There must be a coal chute somewhere; all we have to do is find it. No one would have scrambled up a pile of coal in order to bolt the doors from the inside.'

He heard the sound of the other group returning and waited for them to join him. 'No luck, Sam?'

'No, sir, but we know where they are. At least we know where some of them are. They're in the drawing room. The shutters are closed, but we could hear them laughing and carrying on. I don't think either Miss Fox or Miss Sarah were in there with them.'

Fletcher's heart lurched. This could be good news or the worst possible. 'Was that bastard Wydale in the drawing room? Did you hear his voice?' He knew this was a futile question, how could Sam possibly pick out an individual voice through the muffling wall of shutters and heavy curtains?

'I don't know Mr Reed. But at least they're not at the back of the house and we can get on with finding our way in.'

Roberts shattered the night with a shout of triumph. 'It's over here, sir, I've found it. And you're quite right, it's unlocked.'

Fletcher followed the voice through the darkness and indicated that they all hold their lanterns aloft whilst Roberts and Denver heaved the two doors apart.

He shone his lantern down in to the shining blackness but couldn't see the floor of the coal cellar. Unfortunately there had been a recent delivery and the fuel came almost to the roof. He was about to turn away in disgust when Roberts handed his lantern to Denver.

'I reckon I can slide down that, sir, and then I'll see if I can open the door. With someone in the house it shouldn't be too difficult to let the rest of you in.'

Before Fletcher could forbid it, the young man gathered up his riding coat, shoved his pistol in his pocket, and throwing himself flat slid feet first into obscurity.

They gathered round listening to the crashes, rattles, grunts and cursing as Roberts traversed the mountain of fuel. His passage sent clouds of dust into the air making them all cough.

Eventually the noise stopped and Fletcher held his breath. He sighed with relief as the cheerful voice echoed up from below. 'That was a mite uncomfortable, sir, but I'm down without mishap. I don't suppose one of you would care to push a lantern down to me?'

Edmund's chuckle was weak, but perceptible. 'Don't be a fool, man, you'll set yourself and the whole house alight. You must grope your way to the edge and find the door.'

Thomas stepped forward. 'Excuse me, but that won't be necessary, sir, I got a tinderbox and candles in my pocket, I always travel with them for when the lanterns go out. I can toss them down to him; they'll not light anything on their own.'

'Good man. Do it. Let's hope they don't become lost in the coal.'

'If we all hold our lanterns up by the entrance when your coachman throws the items, Fletcher, with any luck Roberts will see where they go and be able to find them.'

After a deal of scrabbling and swearing Roberts had both tinderbox and candle in his possession. Wisely he stepped away from the gleaming pile of coal before he lit the candle. Fletcher heard the footsteps fade and then a triumphant shout and the small glimmer of a candle appeared at the bottom of the hole.

'I've found the door, it's not bolted on the outside, it's a key. But it's heavy, I can't shift it on my own. In fact I think it will take several men to break it open.'

Fletcher didn't hesitate. He was twice the weight of Roberts, and was sure he could kick the door down, especially the way he felt. Without hesitation he swirled his cloak around him, pulling the collar up to cover his face, and then launched himself feet first, the way Roberts had, down the slippery heap. The speed with which he descended was double that of the groom and he landed in a heap on the floor seconds later.

He heard a startled exclamation and the room went dark. 'Buggeration, I've dropped the candle. I'll never find it in here. It's black as a coal cellar.' This remark caused a ripple of mirth around the men standing on the top.

Fletcher struggled to his feet, his boots slipping on the lumps of coal. 'Don't worry about it, I have another in my pocket. Stay where you are, keep talking and I'll walk towards you. I take it you still have the tinderbox?'

'That I do, sir, I'm not a nodkin.'

Fletcher doubted the veracity of this statement, but his throat was too full of coal dust to answer. Roberts took the candle-end and, expertly using the tinderbox, immediately had a small flame burning. He held it above his head. 'Look, there's the door.'

Fletcher stared and pushing his coat back behind his shoulders in order to leave him free of any hindrance, he took a deep breath. Raising his boot he smashed it down with such force that the lock splintered and the door swung back. He wished it had been Wydale's face beneath his heel.

He was glad to be out of the choking dust and into the comparative fresh air of the narrow passageway. Holding this small flame in front he stared in both directions. He swore viciously. It was like a rabbit warren and he had no real idea in which direction to go to find the back door. Still cursing silently he turned back to speak to the men waiting outside when there was a clatter and a cloud of dust enveloped him.

'Thank God, hear that, Roberts, I think they're all arriving the same way we did.'

Ten minutes later they were assembled in the corridor, the five remaining candle stumps lit and pistols gripped in their hands, all ready to move.

Fletcher was concerned the weapons would no longer fire successfully. Although all had had the sense to push them back into the pockets of their coats during their slide down the coal, it was very likely some dust had got into the firing mechanism and they wouldn't work. There was nothing he could do about it now, it was too dark.

He stood for a moment, trying to visualize the shape of the house. The drawing room, according to Sam, had been on the far side of the building. Leading his band of coal-covered men, coughing and spluttering as they went, he hoped there would soon be stairs leading up to the main part of the house.

He had given instructions that each man was to examine the panelled walls for

266

entrances and if they found one to look inside in case it was the staircase they sought. After ten minutes Edmund shouted triumphantly. 'Here, we've found the stairs.'

Fletcher ran back to join him and resumed his place at the head of the line. A candle in one hand and a pistol in the other, his caped coat flapping around him gave off further clouds of coal dust and caused the men behind a deal of aggravation.

As he reached the top of the winding stairs he could see a band of light shining under the doorway. 'Extinguish your candles, men, we're there.'

He moved forward, slowly pushing the door open a crack, he could feel the men behind freeze like him, listening. There was total silence, no voices, no laughs, nothing.

He shoved the door open and stepped out into a corridor illuminated by a series of flickering flambeaus. This was not the main part of the house, perhaps this passageway was one that led to a study, or an estate office.

'Check your pistols, everybody; see that they are free of dust before we proceed any further.' He did the same himself. As far as he could see everything was working satisfactorily. 'The main entrance must be to our right. Edmund, you keep behind me, Sam and your

267

men follow, then Denver and Roberts and Thomas after that.'

Knowing he had organized his small army as best he could he moved forward, stopping every few yards to listen, but the house was eerily silent. After a few minutes they arrived in the large entrance hall, this too was well lit, but this too was deserted.

However, sounds of raucous laughter and the high-pitched squeals of women were clearly audible through the double doors ahead. He gestured to Edmund to stay with him and sent Sam and his two cohorts to find the servant's entrance. The other three slipped away to find the dining room, so they could approach that way. He would go in through the double doors. If Wydale was there he would shoot him through the heart.

20

Fletcher gave the others five minutes to find the entrance and their places and then flung the doors open. He stood shocked, surveying the room. His eyebrows shot up under his hair at what could be a scene from a Roman orgy. Semi-naked women and men with their britches around their knees were cavorting all over the carpet and furniture. One man glanced casually in his direction and his screech of horror alerted the rest.

Fletcher had been about to shout instructions to these men and their partners to regain their feet and move into the centre of the room, but to his astonishment the room fell silent of its own accord and eight faces, mouths agape, stared at him as if he were the very devil himself.

Before he could move, the servants' door crashed open and then the communicating doors from the dining room did likewise. The eight heads jerked from side to side like marionettes and like marionettes they slowly collapsed.

Fletcher understood why his appearance had caused such consternation. If he looked remotely like the six men who had just emerged then he was a frightening sight indeed. He had forgotten they were all covered in coal, their faces black like sweeps, their clothes exuding clouds of dust as they walked. He tried not to cough and spoil the effect he had created.

Ignoring the pathetic bundles quivering on the floor he called across the room to Sam's group. 'Take an entrance each — guard these creatures; shoot if they so much as blink any resistance.' He beckoned to the others. 'The rest of you come with me, our quarry is not here and we must find him immediately.'

Leaving the debauchery he strode from the room followed by his men. They gathered in the tiled entrance hall.

'I think we had better search upstairs. I imagine Miss Fox and Miss Sarah will have rooms on the first floor. We've no idea where Wydale and his henchmen are so we had better be wary. I shall lead the way: Edmund take your place behind me, then Denver and Thomas bring up the rear.'

Like the other passageways the hall was sufficiently well illuminated to allow them to move forward without recourse to igniting candles. Fletcher led his band forward stealthily, keeping his eyes and ears open.

On reaching the landing halfway up he

gestured to the others to flatten themselves against the wall and remain silent. Then he heard something. Was his mind playing tricks? He cocked his head to listen again. Somewhere ahead a man's voice was raised in anger.

'It's him, he's somewhere upstairs. We outnumber him by far, but he has the advantage if either of the girls are in his clutches. Whatever you do, don't react unless I give the signal.'

A murmur of assent greeted this. Pleased his impromptu troop of foot-soldiers responded so readily to his orders, Fletcher continued upwards. On reaching the head of the stairs he dropped to a crouching position, believing that anyone standing in the passage would automatically look to shoulder height, which might give them the few seconds' advantage they needed to spring an ambush.

He remained still for a second. Wydale, or someone else, continued to berate his victim. He straightened and took the last three steps in one to emerge, poised to kill.

There was no one there. Where were the voices coming from? It wasn't in the main thoroughfare. He ran forward on his toes. As he moved towards the rear of the house the shouting became more distinct until he recognized Wydale. Where the devil was he?

He halted in order to listen again.

Yes, of course! He was in one of the servant's passageways, but it must be somewhere close. He waved to Edmund, miming that he should search the wall for the door. The entrance was found almost immediately and he edged his way forward. Putting his ear to the crack he listened.

'Don't stand there snivelling at me, fetch your mistress at once. She has broken her word, she agreed to come down at seven-thirty and it's ten minutes past that time. She might have decided not to keep her promise, but believe me, I am a man of my word.'

Fletcher's face split into a broad grin. Eliza was safe, she must have locked herself into her chambers and managed to keep the bastard out. Thank God! Thank God! He hadn't been too late, no one's life had been ruined apart from the groom lying dead in the stables. He stepped away from the door and moved across to the far side of the wide passage, beckoning his men to follow.

'We all heard that, both Miss Fox and Miss Sarah are safe. Roberts, take Thomas and try and find another way through; we have to block their escape from the far end of that passage. Edmund have your pistol ready, I'm going in to drag that bastard out and teach him what it means to harm someone of mine.'

He realized he had not given instructions to the other two but guessed they would stand guard in the corridor in case they were needed. He paused at the door. He wanted to be quite certain what to expect before he charged in. He had been away from his post barely a minute and Wydale was still talking to the hidden occupant.

'There's no point in telling me lies. Miss Fox is still within that room. My men have been waiting out here since we made the bargain, no one has come out or they would have seen them. So stop lying and tell Miss Fox that she will have more than one death on her conscience before this night is out if she doesn't appear immediately.'

Fletcher raised his hand to charge in, but hesitated as Wydale shouted to his assistants. 'Go and select the prettiest of the women incarcerated in the servants' hall, bring her here. I'm sure Miss Fox will emerge soon enough when she hears the girl screaming.'

Fletcher had heard enough. He turned sideways and shouldered his way through the door cannoning into the unsuspecting Wydale before he had time to react. His arm shot out and with one movement he lifted the man from his feet and ran backwards, taking him out into the corridor before his servants could react.

Edmund snatched a candle from a nearby table and, followed closely by Thomas, raced after the two murderers.

Fletcher ignored them. His concern was to mete out the punishment Wydale deserved. His opponent had recovered from his shock and, unlike him was unencumbered by a heavy riding coat. Like lightning Wydale sprang forward swinging his fist.

Fletcher swayed sideways and the blow went harmlessly past his ear. Raising his left hand he snatched off his coat, flinging it to the floor. Wydale's teeth were bared and he lashed out a second time with wildly flailing arms.

This time Fletcher was ready and ducked. Swinging back his right fist he jabbed it forward catching his opponent in the solar plexus, knocking all the air from his lungs. His left hook connected underneath Wydale's jaw sending him staggering backwards, blood pouring from his mouth where his teeth had gone through his tongue. After that it was easy. Fletcher pounded the man with a series of ferocious blows and added another to Wydale's teeth for good measure.

Within a few minutes the fight was over, Wydale was unconscious and bleeding on the boards. Fletcher stood back, not a vestige of pity in his face. With calm deliberation, he reached into his pocket and withdrew his pistol, slowly he cocked it and raised his hand, pointing the barrel directly at Wydale's black heart.

As his finger started to close around the trigger, an iron grip took his wrist forcing the gun sideways. 'It's over, Fletcher. You've half killed the man with your fists, don't murder him in cold blood.'

For a moment Fletcher fought an inner battle, then his killing rage subsided and common sense took over. He released his fingers, letting the pistol drop harmlessly to the floor.

'You're right, Edmund, it's over. Come we must release the girls and take them home.' He called back to the men waiting in the passageway. 'Go down and release the servants — the women are in the hall, the men must be somewhere close by. I shall leave them to clear up this mess.' He nodded dismissively at the crumpled heap on the floor.

This time they all carried candles and walking the short distance to the inner door he pulled it back and stared at the makeshift barricade. Why wasn't Eliza there to greet him? Instead, one of her serving maids was standing, wringing her hands in abject misery, when he would be expecting her be jumping for joy at her rescue.

'Where's Miss Fox? What's wrong? Tell me at once.'

'I was telling the truth, sir. She left here more than an hour and a half ago; if she didn't go downstairs then I've no idea where she is. Miss Fox must have met with an accident.'

Fletcher watched the woman fight to regain her composure his elation dissipating. He spoke to her quietly. 'How did Miss Fox get out?'

'The dressing room door has bolts on the inside. She went that way, Mr Reed, sir.'

'Go round to the dressing room and let us in.'

The girl nodded and hurried through to the communicating door. Edmund had been standing close behind and he felt the young man's anxiety. He had no comfort to offer; he felt too worried himself.

Striding, one behind the other, the men arrived outside the door just as it was flung open and light flooded the darkness.

'Quickly, tell me in which direction did Miss Fox go?'

'She went . . . I don't know which way she went, sir, because I had to close the door before she lit a candle in case anyone saw.'

'Edmund, go in and reassure Sarah and then escort all three down to the carriage. I shall take Denver and Roberts and find Eliza.' He stood for a moment deep in thought. The corridors wound in several directions so which way would Eliza have gone? She wouldn't have gone the way they'd just come because she would have been captured. She had to have gone the other way.

'Right, I shall walk down the centre holding the light — one of you press the wall on the right side the other on the left. If there's a hidden door we shall find it.' He was about to leave when Ann hurried back an oil-lamp in her hand.

'Here, Mr Reed, sir, take this, it gives better light than a candle.'

Gratefully he took it and, leading his men, set off to look for his darling girl. He was not a religious man, was not given to making frequent requests to the Almighty, but rather felt he had become over-familiar with his Maker this past twenty-four hours.

They reached the corner and followed it round, he had only gone a couple of yards when he spotted something lying on the floor. His heart contracted with fear. It was a candlestick and a puddle of material. These had to be items Eliza had dropped.

He rushed forward and dropped to his knees to examine them. The cloth was a reticule, and he could feel the hard shape of a pistol within its depths. He knew there was something horribly wrong.

Without standing up he threw out his arm. The wall moved as the hidden doorway was revealed. Springing up he held his lamp aloft. For a moment he could see nothing, then he made out the shape of a dark spiral staircase that must lead down to the servants' hall.

He passed the lamp over his shoulder to Denver. 'Hold it up and keep close. I'm sure we've found her.'

Taking the stairs three at a time he saw a glimmer of golden material ahead. Holding on to the wall for support he looked round and there she was, in a huddle, her face deathly pale and her lovely fair hair a mass of blood.

21

Pushing himself away from the much needed support of the wall, Fletcher stepped over Eliza's body and dropped to his knees. He pressed his fingers under her chin, where a physician friend had once told him you could find a pulse if the person lived. Her skin was cold and clammy and for an awful moment he thought he was too late. Then he forced himself to continue, he had to be sure.

Oh yes! Thank the good Lord! He felt it, a faint, but regular rhythm, under his fingertips. 'She's alive, but barely. Give me your stocks, both of you, between them I can make some sort of bandage. There was the sound of rustling and two limp strips of cloth dropped into his lap.

He should have realized the wound was still oozing blood — if Eliza had been dead this would have ceased. His horror at seeing her unconscious had caused his limited medical knowledge to desert him. He was about to construct a makeshift bandage, but looked down at the material in his hands and saw it was thick with coal dust. Putting these upon an open wound could only exacerbate matters. Tossing them to one side he slid his arms underneath her inert form and scooped her up.

'I'll have to take her back to the chamber. I need clean water and linen. Hurry man, back up, hold the light high so that I can see my feet.' Scarcely five minutes after he had left Edmund to see to his younger sister he returned, Eliza unconscious in his arms.

He stepped into the dressing room and came face-to-face with both of them. Fletcher saw the girl's face drain of colour and her wail of distress made him flinch. 'She's not dead, sweetheart, she's unconscious. She has a bad cut on her head which I'm going to sort out for her. Step aside, there's a good girl, and let me get through.' In the bedroom he was faced by the companion and the other woman. Luckily they immediately understood the seriousness of the situation.

Jane, stepped forward. 'Lay her on the bed, sir, and I'll fetch clean water and cloths.'

He did as she suggested and, whilst waiting for her to return, quickly felt Eliza's limbs for fractures. He even ran his hands around her ribs to make certain none was splintered. Last year a stable boy at Grosvenor Square had drowned in his own blood when a broken rib punctured his lungs.

'Would you like me to do this, sir? I've

been tending Miss Sarah and her cuts and bruises for many years.'

Fletcher was going to refuse, to insist on doing it himself, but remembered his hands were ingrained with coal and it would be better if someone clean dealt with the wound.

He stepped aside and watched helplessly as the two women deftly cleansed the gash that stretched right across Eliza's forehead. How the hell had she managed to fall backwards and then strike the front of her head? He felt sick to his stomach as he reconstructed what must have occurred.

She had somersaulted and landed face first. He shuddered at the thought of the force involved in such a fall. Eliza had been lying almost on her back; the momentum must have caused her to twist a second time until she ended up against the wall. She had been unconscious and losing blood for far too long. He knew how serious things were.

'There, that's all we can do now. Miss Fox urgently needs the attention of a physician, sir, but I've no idea where we would find one around here.'

'Neither do I, and I have no intention of searching. I have my carriage outside. It's barely an hour's journey to my own estate. I shall send my man ahead to rouse the doctor and he will be waiting for us when we arrive.

The sooner we leave these premises the better.'

★ ★ ★

Eliza opened her eyes, but it was night so she closed them again. She was completely disorientated, had no idea where she was or why her head hurt so abominably and every bone in her body ached. She attempted to move her head, but a searing pain across her forehead made her gasp and she stopped.

She wasn't on the floor; it was too soft and comfortable underneath. She tried wiggling her fingers and detected soft linen — she now knew that she was in a bed, and in her night-rail. But whose bed was this? She lay still for a moment trying to make sense of things.

She remembered escaping from the bed-chamber, remembered inching her way along a pitch-dark passageway, and yes, she remembered tumbling backwards. However, she had no recollection of being carried to this bedroom or anything else that followed.

Had Wydale placed her here? Had her plans come to nothing? Surely even the devil himself would not violate an unconscious woman? Eliza lay still, letting her breathing slow. As the heavy thumping of her heart became less she began to hear another sound which filled her with horror. She could hear someone breathing close by. She knew at once what it was: that monster had decided to thoroughly ruin her and was in the bed as well. Ignoring her injuries she clenched her fist and lashed out sideways. Her knuckles connected satisfactorily with solid flesh.

The shout of pain told her she had made a dreadful mistake. She recognized the cry. 'Fletcher? I'm so sorry I thought it was . . . well, you know who I thought it was . . . lying beside me.'

She heard him laughing, totally unfazed by her violence. 'My darling girl, you cannot know how delighted I am to hear your voice. A black eye is a small price to pay to know you're recovered.'

Before she could protest the bed moved and his arms slid around her. His attempt to gather her close was so painful she couldn't help the whimper of pain escaping. Immediately he let her go.

'I'm sorry, darling, does your head hurt very much? You have been unconscious for four days. I was so relieved that you have come round I forgot all about your injury.'

'Where am I, Fletcher? This is not Winterton Hall?'

'Of course not, it's my estate. We brought

you here to be looked after. Your mama and grandmamma are also here and eagerly waiting to see you. I'll go and fetch them.'

'Don't be ridiculous, Fletcher. It's the outside of enough that you're lolling about on my bed in the middle of the night, I certainly don't want my mother and grandmother to witness my disgrace.'

She heard a sharp intake of breath and felt him stiffen. What had she said to upset him? Then his hands brushed over her face, touching her eyes gently. He shuffled closer, this time not moving her, but bringing himself near enough so that he could offer comfort.

'Darling, I have to tell you that it's midday, the shutters are drawn back, the sun is streaming into the room. It's not dark.'

For a second she didn't understand. 'My God! Fletcher, I am blind. I cannot bear it. Never to be able to see the faces of those I love, for ever dependent, like Sarah — like a child being led around the place.' She felt the hot tears trickle down her cheeks and she buried her face in the softness of his shirt.

'I shall fetch Mrs Fox. She can sit with you until the doctor arrives. I'm sure this is only temporary, when you suffer a serious injury it might well take some time for the effects to go.'

Eliza heard the swish of a dress and realized that they hadn't been alone in her bedroom at all.

'Miss Fox, here, let me dry your tears. Would you like a drink of lemonade? It is far too long since you ate or drank anything.'

Eliza recognized Ann's voice. 'Yes, lemonade would be most acceptable, thank you.' She heard Fletcher leaving the room and knew it had to be all over between them. She could never marry him now, whatever they both might wish. A blind wife was worse than no wife at all.

The physician explained that temporary blindness was not unusual and that with time her sight would return, but she didn't believe him. She was totally blind, not even a glimmer of light to give her hope that one day she would see again. She had been prepared to sacrifice her purity, but giving up her vision was almost too much to bear.

⋆   ⋆   ⋆

Her mother had made soothing statements and talked happily about a June wedding, and that as soon as they were home at Grove House they could start preparing her trousseau and organizing the wedding breakfast. Eliza was too dispirited to disabuse her parent.

She would speak to Fletcher, tell him that she could not marry him unless she recovered her sight, but she was enjoying his company too much to spoil things. He had told her what happened at Winterton Hall and how Lord Wydale had been left in the care of his servants. She was glad that the monster was still living — albeit with several teeth missing and a few broken bones.

It was becoming harder and harder to pretend that everything was as it should be, that she too was eagerly anticipating their nuptials. Three days after she had recovered consciousness she was allowed to get up and sit in the pretty, well-appointed sitting room, with a rug over her legs, and receive her visitors there.

Edmund had departed for Grove House the previous day, eager to take on his responsibilities as estate manager. These past three weeks had worked a miracle in her brother. He no longer wished to gad about town gambling and being involved with loose women. His head was full of the innovations he would enact to the farms, and the way he would improve their home in order to make things easier for her.

It was time to tell the man she loved of her decision. When he arrived midmorning carrying a bunch of fragrant hothouse flowers she knew she could postpone it no longer.

'My dear, please sit down, there is something I have to say to you and I know you're not going to like it.'

She heard his sharp intake of breath and believed that he had guessed what she was going to say. She raised her hand to stop him interrupting her. 'Whatever you wish, I cannot marry you as I am. A blind wife is no use to anyone and I refuse to spend my life being led around a strange place by the hand, like a baby in leading strings. If I remain at home at least I shall be able to find my way about without assistance.' He dropped to his knees beside her and attempted to take her hands. She thrust them under the cover, out of his reach.

'Then we shall live at Grove House, my darling girl. It makes no matter to me where I live, as long as I am your husband and can take care of you. I love you, Eliza, it makes no difference to me whether you can see or not.'

'I know how you feel, my love, and I feel the same way. I love you with all my heart, but it's because I love you so much that I cannot marry you. I cannot raise your children as they should be raised; I cannot run your house, or be your hostess. You need someone else at your side: I am not the woman for you any more.'

She heard him swallowing and almost

changed her mind. Instead she turned her head away, knowing that his heart was breaking even as hers was. He didn't try to persuade her to change her mind. She heard him leave the room, but didn't move until he'd gone. She managed to hold back her grief until she was sure he was out of earshot, but then, rolling over, she buried her face in the back of the *chaise-longue* soon soaking it with her tears.

Ann told her that he had left, saying he had business to attend to in town but would visit her to see how she did when she was back at Grove House. She knew he would never come back, she had dismissed him twice. No man returned to be rejected a third time, not even someone who loved her as much as Fletcher. He had his pride after all.

Strangely no one tried to persuade her to change her mind, everyone appeared to accept her decision. She had expected her mother to protest, to wring her hands, to beg her to reconsider, but she appeared sanguine. Her only comment was that Eliza was old enough to make up her own mind and whatever she did, it would be accepted by the rest of the family.

22

It was high time they all returned to Grove House. Her cruelty had driven Fletcher away, sent him up to London to face a barrage of questions from his cronies about what had transpired at Winterton Hall and he hadn't protested. He'd left them in residence in his own home without a murmur.

'Mama, I wish to return home today. I am quite well enough to travel. I know it's a long way, but we can overnight somewhere if you wish. Ann is quite capable of taking care of me, and Jane takes care of Sarah. All you have to do is look after Grandmamma.'

'Very well, Eliza, if that's what you wish to do. I know I should be glad to be back in my own home. Hendon Manor is all very well, but it's not Grove House. It's far too big and I don't know the names of the staff. Fletcher left his coach at our disposal and we don't have a lot of baggage, so I suppose we could be ready to leave later this morning. However, if we depart at first light tomorrow, and take things slowly, stopping once or twice for refreshments and to allow our horses to rest, I think we could accomplish the journey quite easily before teatime and not be obliged to overnight at a coaching inn.'

Eliza didn't care either way; she just wanted to go home. She felt alien in this place; she had never seen it, indeed would never see it, and was scared to venture anywhere apart from around her bedchamber and parlour.

The journey was accomplished remarkably smoothly, everything went as it should, refreshments were waiting for them at their stops, and nowhere was Eliza made to feel uncomfortable or the centre of unpleasant attention.

She felt the coach turn into the long narrow drive that led down to Grove House and her misery lifted a little. This was not the way she'd hoped to come home. She should be happy that neither she nor Sarah had lost their reputation, Edmund and Fletcher had emerged unscathed, only the poor groom had been harmed. Apart from Lord Wydale, of course, but he didn't count. He deserved all the punishment he'd received.

Edmund was waiting at the front door to greet them and embraced her fondly. He had grown up. He was a man, more than ready to take on the responsibility of a houseful of dependent women; at least that was one thing less to worry about.

'Edmund, I'm so pleased to see you . . . '
She choked, she would have to stop saying
the word *see*, but what else could one say?

Edmund chuckled. 'Liza, you will soon be
able to see as well with your ears and your
fingers as someone with sight. You're a
resourceful woman. I'm sure that in a very
short space of time you will hardly notice
your lack of vision.'

After a flurry of greetings she was escorted
up to her room. She had no time to ponder
on his words, but when she was comfortable
and settled in her bed, her own possessions
around her, she relaxed and thought about
his statement.

Would she become accustomed to being
unsighted? She had to admit that already her
hearing had sharpened and she tended to feel
things in order to discover what they were.
She still had her music — she had no need
for eyes to play the pianoforte. Perhaps life
would not be so empty after all. She knew
that was untrue for without her love she was
truly lost.

Sarah had promised to be her guide, to
lead her around the garden and tell her
everything there was to see. Indeed her sister
was the only one who seemed happy with the
new circumstances. Sarah finally had a role to
play, an important duty to perform, and all

thought of leaving to be a princess was forgotten. She seemed to have accepted her position in the household and was content with it.

★ ★ ★

Weeks passed and Eliza began to smile a little and regain her appetite but she missed Fletcher so much. He had promised to come and visit, to see how she did, but she didn't expect him to.

The occupants of Grove House were inordinately cheerful, considering the circumstances. Why was everyone so happy? Sometimes it made her quite cross to see how little anyone thought of her misery. To have lost the man she loved a second time, as well as her sight, surely deserved more sympathy? But, when she fingered her way towards a room, she could often hear the sound of suppressed laughter, and she'd heard unidentified voices several times. However, no one had seen fit to inform her who they were and she had no intention of asking.

The vicar had been up to see her, although she didn't feel ready to attend church yet, and said everything that was proper, but he also didn't seem to take the fact that she was going to remain a miserable spinster the rest of her life as seriously as she expected.

She realized finally that being blind, although a serious handicap, was not half as painful as living without the man she loved. She had to be strong, for both of them. Every night she dreamt about having his dear arms around her again, but she would not weaken. It was up to her to be strong, she repeated this to herself again and again, hoping to convince herself she had not made a disastrous error.

★ ★ ★

Towards the end of the month the weather turned warm and everyone was talking about there being a good summer on its way. Her mother had taken to leaving her bedchamber window open to allow fresh air in and for her to be able to hear the nightingales singing in the park.

'Mama, all my life you've been telling me it's injurious to one's health to have windows wide open at night. What has happened to make you change your mind?'

'I have been speaking to Dr Smith, my dear, and he said that as you're not going outside as much as you were used to I was to ensure that you got fresh air in other ways.'

Eliza had to be satisfied with this

prevarication. However, she enjoyed the breeze and liked to hear the curtains moving gently across the polished boards.

Not long after this conversation she retired and, as usual, failed to sleep. Her longing for Fletcher had not abated one jot and she was seriously considering sending a message to him asking him to visit. She heard her mantel clock chime midnight before she eventually fell into a restless slumber.

*   *   *

Fletcher waited until it was quite dark and all the lights were extinguished before approaching Grove House. He'd walked up from the town, leaving his baggage at the Sun along with his manservant, Sam. It was his intention to break into the house tonight like a burglar. He grinned knowing that he was indeed a thief, because he had come to steal something precious.

This clandestine visit had been arranged with her family before he left Hendon Manor so many lonely days ago. It had been agony staying away from her, but he knew it would be foolish to appear too soon — he had to be sure she was as miserable as he at their separation.

He crept round to the front of the house

and stared up at the open window on the first floor, knowing it was Eliza's room, hers was the only bedchamber with a balcony. He scaled the height of the wall without difficulty. Tonight he was lucky and the silvery light of the moon made his ascent easy.

He dropped lightly in his stockinged feet over the balustrade. He smiled at the thought of his boots being discovered untenanted on the front doorstep next morning. Both French doors were firmly jammed open; the arrangement had been that one door would be left slightly ajar to allow him to enter, but obviously Mrs Fox was making absolutely sure he could get in without arousing her daughter.

Stepping into the room he stood like a shadow in the corner staring across at the bed. Yes, she was there, fast asleep; he could hear her rhythmic breathing. His eyes filled and he wanted to leap across and snatch her into his arms, covering her face with kisses.

Instead he crept across into the dressing-room where he swiftly removed all his garments. Only then did he stealthily approach the bed and, pulling back the covers, slid in beside his beloved totally unclothed. He had no intention of pre-empting their wedding night, just making absolutely certain that she would have to marry him, whatever her reservations about her handicap. It had all been arranged to allow her no escape. Mrs Fox would arrive first thing in the morning as if wishing to speak to Eliza and find him in bed with her. That would be more than enough.

Eliza's mother had promised to make a drama that no one would ever forget. Everyone in the house would hear and the special licence would be produced from his pocket, the vicar fetched and the marriage take place immediately before the disgrace could travel all round the town.

He had to suppress his laughter. One day he would tell Eliza this had been planned by her loving family. They knew, as he did, why she had refused him and also knew that no one would ever convince her she was wrong. They sincerely believed that this unorthodox plan was the only way they could make her happy.

★   ★   ★

Something disturbed Eliza's dream — she was imagining she was in Fletcher's arms, inhaling his lemony scent when her eyes flicked open. She could still smell the distinctive aroma but knew her mind must be playing tricks.

She yawned and rolled over to find a cool place on the sheets. Her squeal of shock when she encountered naked male flesh reverberated around the room. She felt his chest vibrating with amusement.

'Fletcher, what on earth are you doing in my bed with no clothes on?'

'What do you think I am doing, my darling? Let me hold you the way I've always longed to. I know you won't marry me — I'm not asking you to — but let me put my arms around you just this once. Give me something to remember. I promise I shall be gone long before anyone discovers me here.'

This was ridiculous. What a shocking suggestion. Eliza drew breath to refuse but she couldn't. Somehow her prayers had been answered and who was she to argue with the Almighty? Without a word she closed the distance between them and slid her arms around his neck. She didn't care that he had no clothes on, didn't care that her feet became entangled between his naked legs. All she wanted was to feel him next to her, taste his mouth on hers just once more.

A few breathless moments later, Fletcher enquired softly, 'It doesn't seem fair, my darling, that you can explore my skin and I cannot do the same. Shall I remove this voluminous garment?'

Without a murmur she raised her arms and he tugged her nightgown up over her head and tossed it casually to one side. He pulled her back into his arms and Eliza felt she was exactly where she belonged. All her reservations about their union dissolved under his tender tutelage.

When they eventually fell asleep, even she could not deny that they were meant to be together and that in the circumstances it would be best if their wedding took place as soon as possible.

The following morning Eliza opened her eyes horrified to see that it was already light and that her lover was still beside her. She had no wish to shock her mother by her outrageous behaviour. It would be better by far if everyone thought she had had a change of heart and Fletcher appeared later in the day as if having been summoned at her request.

She was about to wake him with a gentle kiss when she screamed instead. He jack-knifed awake, his face shocked by her outburst.

'Fletcher, the sun is up, the room is full of sunlight.' She waited for his sleep-befuddled brain to register the import of her words.

Slowly his mouth curved into a smile of comprehension. 'Sweetheart, I didn't think life could get any better. How much can you see?'

'Your outline, light and shade, not everything, but after being in total darkness for three weeks it's a miracle that I can see anything at all.' She fell back into his arms and covered his face with kisses.

It was hardly surprising that, in the circumstances, Fletcher completely forgot the arrangement he had made with his future mother-in-law.

THE END

We do hope that you have enjoyed reading
this large print book.

Did you know that all of our titles
are available for purchase?

We publish a wide range of high quality
large print books including:
Romances, Mysteries, Classics
General Fiction
Non Fiction and Westerns

Special interest titles available in
large print are:
The Little Oxford Dictionary
Music Book
Song Book
Hymn Book
Service Book

Also available from us courtesy of Oxford
University Press:
Young Readers' Dictionary
(large print edition)
Young Readers' Thesaurus
(large print edition)

For further information or a free
brochure, please contact us at:
Ulverscroft Large Print Books Ltd.,
The Green, Bradgate Road, Anstey,
Leicester, LE7 7FU, England.
Tel: (00 44) 0116 236 4325
Fax: (00 44) 0116 234 0205

Other titles published by
The House of Ulverscroft:

LORD THURSTON'S CHALLENGE

Fenella-Jane Miller

When Charlotte Carstairs and her sister and brother are made orphans she seeks out her estranged grandfather, Lord Thurston. However, Major Jack Griffin has inherited the title and will allow Charlotte and her family to remain at Thurston on the condition that she is able to improve the house and estate, which are in ruins. Charlotte, determined to stay, persuades Lord Thurston to take a proper interest in his property. Then as his interest turns to her they grow closer, but sinister forces work to ruin their plans. Can they unmask the murderous plotters before losing everything?

THE MESALLIANCE

Fenella-Jane Miller

Lady Allegra Humphry, being at the top of the aristocratic tree, has no time for *cits* — suitors from the merchant class. But she and her brother, Richard, the Earl of Witherton, must make compromises if they are to retain their position in society. Self-made millionaire Silas Tremayne now owns Allegra's ancestral home, and is determined to own her as well. Rejected by the *haut ton* , Silas plans to ensure both he and his daughter, Demelza, will be welcome in the best drawing-rooms. Marriage is the answer! But there are people against the union, and those who are prepared to commit murder to stop it . . .